INTO THE NIGHT
AND OTHER STORIES

Johnny Carless, charismatic criminal owner of an all-night café in Merseyside, is cunning but prone to explosions of rage. Confronting a subordinate who has defected and betrayed his activities to a rival, Carless loses control. He pulls his gun and fires, continuing shooting as the dying man crashes through a window into the street outside. Forced to go on the run, Carless escapes to London. There, he meets an innocent and beautiful girl, who falls for his charms — and becomes reluctantly embroiled in his criminal activities . . .

NORMAN FIRTH

INTO THE NIGHT

And Other Stories

Complete and Unabridged

LINFORD
Leicester

First published in Great Britain

First Linford Edition
published 2016

Copyright © 1946, 1947 by Norman Firth
Copyright © 2015 by Sheila Ings

A catalogue record for this book is available
from the British Library.

ISBN 978–1–4448–2735–4

Published by
F. A. Thorpe (Publishing)
Anstey, Leicestershire

Set by Words & Graphics Ltd.
Anstey, Leicestershire
Printed and bound in Great Britain by
T. J. International Ltd., Padstow, Cornwall

This book is printed on acid-free paper

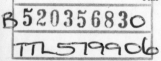

Contents

Into the Night

1

Johnny Carless

The dump was in a narrow stinking street known to all and sundry as Mugs Alley. That wasn't the right name of the street, but they called it that because it was crammed from end to end with pin table saloons, pool halls, and gambling joints. More people had themselves rooked there than anywhere else on Merseyside.

The dump was called 'Johnny's Joint' and the majority of the smart boys hung out there. It was an all-night eatery with a special Blue Plate. It didn't close ever, and it was run by none other than Johnny Carless, who'd been making his living out of suckers ever since he was ten.

It didn't have a good reputation with the cops; but they never found out about the gambling hall back of the dump. This night it wasn't so crowded. It was about ten-thirty, and outside in the dismal damp darkness of the street the pin table joints were doing a roaring trade. But Johnny's eatery wasn't.

That was kind of funny in itself.

Johnny's was almost always crowded; but — maybe the wise boys along the street had heard there was going to be trouble!

Anyway, only a few mugs and suckers, who weren't regular patrons of the dump, were there that Thursday night. Them and the ten boys who comprised Johnny's strong-arm men.

As if they were waiting for something, they sat silently at the tables in the alcoves, and they talked in low tones, but their eyes kept travelling towards the door, and once or twice they'd look over at Johnny who stood propping up the bar with his forearms, not saying anything to anybody and not giving a look at his boys, just staring blankly in front of him at the mirror that hung back of the bar, through which he could lamp the doorway!

Suddenly he stiffened up, turned, and went across the room at what was almost a run, his long legs carrying him into the street.

There was a little runt just slinking past the end of the dump's windows.

'Hey, Smeller,' called Johnny, hastening after him.

The little runt known as Smeller seemed uncertain whether to head on or whether to stop.

Johnny reached him, said: 'Ain't you steppin' inside tonight, Smeller?'

The runt eyed him with a touch of fear.

'I — er — I reckon not, Johnny.'

'You *ought* to, pal,' stated Johnny. 'You look like you could do with a good stiff drink. You're tremblin'!'

'I — I guess maybe I've got a touch of cold through the damp weather,' mumbled Smeller.

'You got a touch of cold, all right,' agreed Johnny. 'But it ain't through no weather. What you got is *cold feet!*'

The runt coughed nervously: 'I gotta go now, Johnny.'

'Sure you have — you gotta go right inside the eatery.'

'I tell ya I ain't got time.'

'You're goin', just the same. You'll have to find time.'

Plucking up courage from some place the runt said: 'Who says so? If I say I don't wanna go, who's gonna make me go?'

Johnny said: '*This*, pal.'

The runt went, and he didn't argue anymore either. He hadn't been kicking round the rackets so short a time he didn't know what the bulge in Johnny's pocket was. He went inside the saloon, and Johnny said: 'Get over at that table with the boys. They'll be right pleased to see you.'

Smeller got over; the boys said: 'Well, if it ain't Smelly, back again!'

'We figured you'd resigned, Smelly.'

'Sure. Nice to see you back.'

Quivering like an undersized jelly, Smeller hit the seat of a chair with the seat of his pants. He sat still, his eyes shifting from one to another of the mob.

Johnny yelled to the hash slinger back of the counter.

'Close the joint up.'

The hash slinger said: 'Sure, Johnny. But how about the mugs that ain't finished yet?'

'Get them out, anyway. They'll have to leave what they ain't ate. Don't charge 'em.'

The hash slinger bawled: 'Okay, gents, get the wind in your behinds. We're closin' up.'

A small character with horn-rimmed gig-lamps grunted: 'What do you mean, closing up? It says plain outside this is an all-night eatery!'

'I said we're closin' up. Scram — '

'I haven't finished yet.'

One of the boys got up and came over. He stared down at the small man in spectacles, then at the girl with him. He looked almighty mean about something. The girl, young and blonde and on the ingenuous side, shivered. The small character looked up at him nervously, then muttered: 'If a place says it's an all-night eatery, it should stay open, shouldn't it, mister? That cheap bum behind the counter can't heft us out until we've finished, can he?'

The man deliberately shoved away the small character's plate. He snarled: 'You tryin' to be big in front of your floozie, pal?'

'I — er — no, no, I'm not. But — '

'Don't *but* me, mister. I get sore. Do like the nice man says before I use my hands on you! Beat it! See? Before I get good and sore.' And he leaned and spat deliberately in the small character's face.

The girl pleaded, hoarsely: 'Hubert, dear, do let's get out.'

Hubert produced a silk handkerchief and mopped saliva from the lens of his goggles. He placed them back on his nose and started to get indignant. He said: 'Call the manager of this establishment! I demand to see the manager.'

Johnny Carless strolled over. He came to rest at the table, said: 'Someone asking for me?'

The gang man grunted. 'Billy told everyone to move like you said. Everyone did — exceptin' for this little skunk. He aims to get clever — kinda show-off, front of his gal.'

Johnny said: 'What's the matter with you? Can't you go nice and peaceable, or do we have to throw you out?'

The mug called Hubert took one look at his face and wilted.

Johnny said: 'You from the University?'

'Ye — yes.'

'Swell — only they got a rule about the students fightin', ain't they? No student is allowed to indulge in fisticuffs, ain't that it? Under pain of expulsion.'

'Yes. They made that rule after the students got mixed up with the dockers last autumn.'

'That so? Interestin'. Well, smart boy, if you don't lam out of here like you been told, and quick, you'll be walkin' into the lecture hall with two black eyes, an' maybe a split nose an' lip come morning. Now what do you say? Go peaceful?'

The college boy got up hastily. Johnny's expression told him trouble was bubbling. His girl got up with him.

Johnny said: 'An' don't try to get fresh in future with strange guys, or next time you might not be so lucky.'

The door closed back of them. Johnny said: 'Okay, Manselm. Lock the door and draw the blinds — you stay where you are, Smeller. We're getting round to you fast.'

The doors were locked, blinds drawn. The eatery became a tiny shut-off world of its own. Anything could happen there — Smeller felt anything *was* going to happen there — to him!

He shifted about uneasily in his chair.

Johnny snapped: 'Sit still, Smeller. You got a flea in your pants?'

Smeller gasped: 'What do you want with me, Johnny? What's all the fuss about? You don't want me.'

Johnny leaned hard knuckles on the table. His grey eyes bored deep into Smeller. He rasped: 'Been a long time since you was in here, Smeller. Five weeks, ain't it?'

'Yes — yep — but — you got my note, didn't you?'

'Sayin' you was throwin' in with Morelli and handin' us the big push?'

'Yeah. I — I figured — seein' Morelli offered me more dough that I'd throw in with him.'

'How come you didn't come round in person to tell me about it? Yeller?'

'I — I figured a note'd serve just as well. I didn't want any trouble.'

'Nope? Well, now you got more trouble than you can handle, smart guy. And what you goin' to do about it?'

'I don't get you. You can get along without me, I guess.'

Johnny smiled, and the boys laughed. Johnny said: 'We *can* get along swell without you. You always was a nuisance, anyway. But you knew too much about *our* rackets to walk into *another* outfit!'

Smeller wheezed: 'I — I wouldn't tell anything . . . you got to believe that, Johnny. I am not any stool — '

He was all tight inside, and his heart was doing flip-flops up and down his stomach. He knew that look on Johnny's face, knew Johnny was getting madder and madder by the way he was smiling.

Johnny grunted: 'Lessee, Smeller . . . one week after you cut away, that stock of pin machines we had stored was bust into, and every one of them smashed to hell with a hammer. That meant we couldn't supply the Irish district with pin tables. But someone did! An' we since find out that someone was Morelli! Now if you'd given Morelli the facts as to where we had them tables in store, he'd break 'em up, knowing that he could supply tables for that section.'

'I didn't, Johnny, honest I didn't.'

'Then maybe you know who did?'

'I — I reckon not. I — '

'There was only my boys knew where we had them hid. We was frightened of someone finding out. You was one of the boys then. It was about that time you left to hitch to Morelli's mob.'

'I — I wouldn't do a thing like that, Johnny. I swear — '

Johnny went on remorselessly. 'Then there was that pack of dope that I get regular from the central dope ring in Birmingham. Only you and the boys knew that that came packed inside the handle of a suitcase, delivered to Al's place to be picked up by a guy who'd call for it. Manselm went to get it as usual, last week. He was hijacked, in the darkness between here and Gordon Avenue. You knew he'd take that route — so did somebody else. Manselm was knocked cold and the dope stolen — five thousand quids' worth of it! My supplies for a month! Manselm couldn't see too clear, but he claimed it was Morelli's boys that done that.

'Then there've been other things Morelli's found out. That old theatre we meant to convert into a swell night spot — he found that out and stepped in ahead of us and bought the place out. That ain't all — but all these things that have happened you knew about. And you were the only one who could have told Morelli — or would have done. So that when Manselm comes down tonight and says he's seen you walking along this street as he was passing in the car, I kinda prepared this here little reception for you — how'd you like it?'

Smeller didn't; he quavered: 'Listen, I didn't tell anythin'. You don't think I'm that kinda heel . . . honest, Johnny — you don't reckon I'd split like that?'

Johnny grunted: 'We don't reckon. We know; know that's why Morelli took you on. Okay. We don't want to start any gang war with Morelli; the cops have tightened up lately. But we ain't going to let you get away with double crossin'.'

Smeller whimpered: 'If you — if you kill me, Morelli'll make you answer for it! I know he will — he said if I told him, nothin' would happen to me — '

'So you *did* tell him, huh? An' you figure he'll protect you? Okay. We'll see about that . . . '

He went to a phone back of the bar. He hooked the ring and dialed a number. He got through, grunted: 'That Morelli?'

He held the earpiece away from his ear so that they could all listen. The thin metallic voice came through: 'Yeah, sure, this is Gigli Morelli. Why? Who's that?'

'Name of Carless,' Johnny told him.

There was a pause, then: 'Johnny Carless? What in hell you got to say to me, Carless?'

Johnny said: 'I know you been hijacking our stuff and jumpin' in on our rackets, Morelli. And I know where you *got* your information. The way it boils down is like this: I don't aim to start any shooting trouble down here. The cops are too warm — but I can't close my eyes to what's been going on. Now I figure you don't want to shoot things out any more than I do so here is my proposition.

'I got Smeller down here — got him tonight. I know he's the rat that spilt our business. I'm goin' to bump him — an' when I've done that we'll let bygones be bygones, and forget about the way you've chiseled good money out of me. Smeller says you'll blast the living daylights out of us if you know we've bumped him. I say you'll forget it if we do. What do you say?'

They could hear Morelli laugh. He said: 'Let's get this straight, Carless. You say if you bump Smeller without me interferin', honour will be kinda satisfied from your point of view, an' you'll forget I muscled in on your territory. Is that so?'

'That's about the size of it. Providin' you agree to steer clear of us in future.'

For a minute there was silence; and then Morelli's voice came over the telephone: 'Okay, Carless, it's a deal. Smeller ain't any use to me anymore, anyway. Go ahead and rub him out. He ain't important from my point of view!'

Smeller yelled: 'Boss — boss, you promised . . . Holy Christ, come and get me — tell him you'll make trouble!'

Rough hands pushed him back to his seat. Morelli asked: 'What was all the yellin' about?'

Johnny grunted: 'Smeller was pleadin' with you to save his skin.'

Morelli laughed harshly. 'Is that all? I figured it was somethin' important!'

Johnny hooked the phone back on the rest. Smeller had gone grey, dirty grey. His eyes swiveled wildly from side to side. He drooled weakly from the sides of his lips, and his fingers shook in his terror.

Johnny got hold of him by the collar, jerked him forward and jammed him back down over the bar. He drew a gun from his pocket. He snarled: 'You get it *here*, Smeller. We can move the body *after*.'

He looked at his gun to see the silencer was fitted right. He stepped back six paces and raised it.

Smeller yelped: 'I'll come back to you Johnny, I'll work for you again — I'll do anythin' — but for Christ's sake don't shoot that iron off — listen, Johnny . . . I can tell you things . . . '

'I don't like double dealers,' Johnny told him. 'Quit squawkin' an' take it like a man, you rat . . . '

He hauled back on the trigger and at the same moment Smeller made a sudden sideways dive, in a last-minute effort to get out. The slug tore into his hip but apart from a scream of pain he kept going. He headed for the windows, over which were the paper blinds.

Johnny snapped: 'Come back, you bastard, come back here! You two-timing little rat, I'll . . . '

He pumped another shot at Smeller's back — it hit just as Smeller, continuing his frantic flight, crashed through the sheet of plate glass, carrying the blinds with him. There was a chorus of screams from passersby, and as Johnny appeared at the break, gun in hand, they howled in terror and cleared hastily away from the moaning, groveling Smeller.

Johnny pumped bullets into him, every one telling. Smeller bled in a great gush from the mouth, and stopped jerking. Johnny heard the shrill blast of a whistle and saw a blue uniformed cop on his way at a rapid run. He fired up and the cop fell with a slug in the knee.

But others were on the way.

Johnny came racing back into the eatery. He shouted: 'Break it up and run like hell. This'll be the death of us — no time to argue and talk. Get going!'

The boys stared at him for one awed minute. Manselm yelled: 'You blasted fool, Johnny, why'd you let your temper run away with you again? You should've let him beat it — we could have got him again.'

Johnny fisted him in the mouth as he passed. He didn't take that kind of talk from anyone. Then the boys were streaming out of the back doors, and splitting up, and running for it.

Johnny lost himself in a maze of alleyways, ran on desperately to the edge of town — alone.

Morning found him riding the rods for London.

2

Fate Slips Up

If anyone had told Johnny Carless things might be preordained, and that there was such thing as Fate to be reckoned with, and that Fate eventually led a man or woman to his or her destiny, he'd have looked them in the eyes without expression and told them they were nuts!

Johnny believed a man controlled his own Fate, and reached his own destiny entirely by his own efforts.

Johnny believed you could play the suckers good and often, and live easy, with a lead percolator for your bosom companion, and not come to any grief provided you didn't stick out your neck too far. His idea was that if he ever was caught — and he doubted the possibility of this in his case — that you had only yourself to blame anyway, and deserved all that was coming to you.

You had to be smarter than the cops; you ruled life and if it went wrong that wasn't Fate — that was your own fault and no one else's.

But Fate was taking a hand in his life right then. He couldn't have stopped it — Fate was planning to bring together him and a girl — a girl called Stella Fraser.

They were on strings, strings of life that Fate manipulated, and maybe originally they weren't meant to meet. But like a couple of puppets in the show of life, Fate jerked them roughly towards each other. Their strings got inexplicably tangled up, and from there on they stayed together, whether they liked it or not.

Johnny Carless had been born on Merseyside, and as a young boy he'd lived and learned the hard way. You can learn more of life around the Liverpool docks than anywhere else in this world.

When he'd been five he used to creep upstairs at nights to the top rooms of the tenement building he lived in with his widowed mother. He'd crept up there because there was a woman who fascinated him; a coarse, heavily rouged and powdered woman, who wasn't like the rest of the toil-worn women in that tenement.

She used to wear loose kimonos, and even at that early age he'd wondered why all the men eyed her like they did, like they were wild animals, straining to keep themselves in check.

He'd sneaked up at nights and crouched outside her door, and listened to her talking to the men who visited her, sailors and navy boys and men of all nationalities. She'd go out about ten o'clock at night, and she'd always come back with a man. And he'd wondered, and kept on wondering, until a glimmering of the truth crept across his infant mind. That was when he'd been five and three months.

There'd been Mrs. Tally, too. She was married, unhappily, to a big, hulking Norwegian labourer. Johnny had often seen him beating her, until her whole coarse body was blue and she was screaming out in pain every time the belt he used fell on her. He'd beaten her at all times, when she was with child, and she always was. He beat the kids as well, the entire ten of them, who lived in three scrubby little rooms.

There'd been a smart boy on the first floor, and he'd been the best dressed in the tenement. He always had lots of dough, and he looked down on everyone else.

He made a friend of the inquisitive Johnny for some reason. And from him Johnny had learned the truth about the bosomy girl on the top floor, and why Mrs. Tally had had ten visits from the stork and his own ma only one.

He learned plenty more as he grew older. How his friend made his money in the rackets, and other things. And by the time he was fifteen he was already on the crooked road from which he was never to escape.

Twenty-one came and went, and his ma died. He left home and threw in his lot with a mob. By the time he was twenty-four, his knowledge of life and ruthlessness had put him in a position to front his own mob.

Strangely enough in spite of — or

perhaps because of — his experiences as a child, he didn't bother with women. He was the only gang leader in that part of the country who didn't. But he was steadfast in his views — he even went so far as to discourage his boys from consorting with the deadly female of the species. He claimed women were *more* trouble —

And so, right up to the time when he'd shot down Smeller and his gang had been split up and lost contact, taking it on the lam, he'd been more or less a lone wolf.

The loss of his boys failed to worry him; he was young and he could make a fresh start.

He was thinking like that the day he arrived in London, after he'd had a brush up and wash in the station there. He was still thinking like that when he strolled aimlessly down Sussex Street, one of the less enviable streets in London's dirty patch.

Meanwhile, at the same time, Stella Fraser was stripping off her neat but cheap clothes and her silk underthings, and running the water for her bath.

Stella Fraser had come from reasonably respectable people who had lived on the outskirts of the city. Her father had been a clerk in a ticket office, and he'd been a thrifty man. He'd pared down housekeeping expenses to a minimum, and he'd begrudged every item of clothing he'd had to buy for his wife and daughter. His growls at every penny that was spent had turned Stella's mother's hair grey. He'd even been annoyed when the wife had insisted on sending Stella to high school, but for once he'd been overruled.

His wife didn't really mind. He had explained that he was saving the money for Stella to have a decent start in life.

When Stella was sixteen — and an extremely pretty and pure sixteen, owing to the fact that she never had the money or clothes to go to any places where she might meet boys of her own age, and she was always so dowdily dressed that the high school boys looked on her as a drip — when she was sixteen her father had walked in front of a tram-car one night while drunk.

After they'd scraped him off the

pavement and packed the bits into a casket, several interesting things came to light.

The most interesting was that he'd been keeping a mistress for more than ten years, and that the money he was supposed to have been saving for his wife and daughter had all gone on her. Not a bent copper remained.

It was a bit too much for Stella's mother. Three nights later Stella had found her with her head in the gas oven and a farewell note by her side, which simply said:

'Stay single, daughter. No man is worth it.'

So that had finished Stella's education, and she'd gone to live with an old uncle over the other side of the city. Unfortunately, it seemed Ebenezer's interest in her had not only been paternal; so, equipped with the knowledge a woman of the world must have to get by, and in possession of a fair share of the answers, she left secretly one night, and vanished from Ebenezer's ken. She vanished as far as Sussex Street where she took a shabby apartment. The great thing about Sussex Street was that its tenements had been originally built for the rich.

That had been way back.

Time had decreed that the fashionable set should move elsewhere. They had moved, and their late resort had deteriorated over a number of years, until its shabby, once ornate buildings could no longer wear their degeneracy with the air of aristocracy, because of their new tenants, the scum of the earth, foreigners, outcasts, and crooks, mingled together. They were the scum of the earth in the opinion of the smart set only. Actually, amongst the heterogeneous collection of creeds and races established in Sussex Street, more kind hearts were to be found than could be found in the so-called upper stratum of English society.

It was here that Stella had found the buxom Mrs. Flannery, typical Irish washerwoman, with rolled sleeves, beefy red arms and a heart as big as her bosom. It was Mrs. Flannery who had decried the suggestion of her bothering her head about the rent until she had a job and steady salary. It was Mrs. Flannery who had fed her during the trying time she had faced.

Mrs. Flannery also had eventually arranged — through a friend of hers, who knew a friend, who knew a friend, whose second cousin's wife's brother-in-law knew a man who ran an office uptown and who needed a stenographer.

Furthermore, when Mrs. Flannery had arranged for her to cinch the job, she had made some very close inquiries from her friend's, friend's, second cousin's, wife's brother-in-law's friend, and had eventually satisfied herself that the man *did* need a secretary, and not a glorified lap-dog.

So Stella had gone to work.

She experienced no desire to move from shabby Sussex Street.

Shabby it might be, but it was cozy. Having been built for the rich it boasted bathrooms; and although the paint was chipped and worn and the porcelain cracked, it was clean, and there was a bath to every set of rooms, which made it all the more attractive.

So she tested the water with her pink

toe, and stepped in. She sang softly as she washed, and Fate was farthest from her mind. Like Johnny she hadn't any idea that the die was cast and her whole life was to change, soon.

* * *

Out in Sussex Street, wandering aimlessly along, Johnny was mapping out his future. He halted on the corner, took stock of his roll. He boasted exactly four five-pound notes.

That was all he had had on him; and when he thought of the thirty-odd thousand he had had to leave behind him when he had lammed out, he gritted his teeth and polluted the atmosphere with a few plain and fancy cuss words.

He quit counting his roll — it was so small it hadn't taken him ten seconds to count it, anyway. He stuffed it into his pants pocket and walked on. He was wondering how he stood in London. Had the Liverpool cops blasted a description and account of the crime out here? Yeah, sure to have. Then wasn't he in danger, walking on a main thoroughfare on a Saturday afternoon, in broad daylight?

He glanced about him. The street was crowded. There were hawkers and barrowmen selling everything from roll-ons to spittoons. There was fruit and groceries and meat in plenty. There was garlic and spinach. California oranges and English tomatoes.

The street was packed to capacity. Even if they did have his description it was hardly likely he'd be spotted in such a crowd. And anyway, he didn't have anything to distinguish him from any ordinary guy. He was tall, he was a good build, he was dark and he wore his hair sleeked back, in black waves.

He wore a small moustache just to show 'em.

He was aware of women eyeing him greedily as he passed. He didn't pause to give one of them a tumble. He kept going. They didn't enter into his scheme of things.

It was right then that he heard the shout!

It came from behind him. It went:

'*Hoy! Buddy! I want you!*'

He stiffened and glanced back over his shoulder. What he saw made him go cold.

A beefy Irish cop was shoving through the crowd, waving a hand at him. His face was red and excited. He was bawling: '*You! Come back here! Mister! You hear me?*'

Johnny picked up his feet and started running, dodging through the mass of people, elbowing them aside. He wasn't concerned where he might wind up — as long as it wasn't with a noose around his neck!

But he knew now they had him tagged; they were looking out for him here.

The cop lumbered behind him, sweating and jostling a way through.

He turned off down a side alley. He got halfway down there and suddenly discovered it was a blind end. He raced for the fire escape on his left.

He had to jump to reach the slide down. But he made it, and with a grating of rust the escape slid towards him. He started climbing well before it had hit the ground, and as he gained the first platform the slide-down ladder slid up again. The cop was just entering the alley.

Johnny went fast up the escape. He heard the cop jump for the slide down too, heard him miss and flop on his back with a wild curse. He kept going on: the cop might make it any minute and it wasn't an opportune time for laughing at the antics of cops, no matter how big and Irish they were.

The escape opened on to some bathrooms; he could see them as he went up the escape. Once he tried the window of one, but it was fast.

Now he could hear the pounding feet of the cop behind him. A few more moments and . . .

He came to a window which was open. A gauze blind flapped back of it. He thrust the blind aside and went in.

The girl who was sitting naked in the bath didn't scream. She just stared at him open-mouthed, then streaked for the towel on the handy rail, and disposed it about her white body. She said:

'*What* is this, exactly?'

He looked at her; snapped: 'Where's

the key to this room?'

She told him: 'Somewhere in my clothes — my costume pocket.'

He hesitated; there was no time to search. He said: 'Listen, and get this right first time: there's a guy following me who I don't want to see. He'll be here in a coupla seconds — them are his flat feet you can hear pounding the irons outside. When he looks in here I'll be hidin' back of the bath. You have to say your piece — you have to say no one came in here — maybe they went right on over the roof!'

She snapped: '*Get out of here!* What do you think I am?'

He produced the gun from his pocket. He said: 'I know what you will be if you don't do it, sister!'

'If you think I'm afraid of *that* — ' she began, and then he bent over her and slapped her hard across the mouth. He snarled:

'If you blow on me I'll plug you before I go — I'm wanted for murder anyway, so one more won't hurt!'

Then the steps outside stopped, and he

32

slid silently back of the bath.

The curtains opened; the cop peered in. Johnny heard him: 'Has a — *wuhoooo!* Say, lady . . . '

He listened with bated breath. If she split —

There was a moment of silence. Then: 'How *dare* you look in here like this? Go away at once before I send for the police!'

'But lady, I *am* the police. See, I'm wearing uniform.'

'Oh, you are, are you? Then oughtn't you to be ashamed of yourself, you peeping Tom? Get away from that window . . . '

The Irish cop said: 'I'm only doin' my dooty, lady.'

'Really? Is it part of your duty to sneak round staring in at girls in their baths?'

'I was chasin' a guy. He hefted up this escape. I didn't see him get off, but since this is the only window I figure he must have gone in here. Is he here, lady?'

'Does it look as though he was?' she sneered coldly. 'Just what do you think this is, officer? Victoria Station on a Saturday afternoon?'

The cop said, sheepishly: 'I could have swore by the beard of St. Patrick he come in here. But it don't look like it . . . know where he might've gone?'

She said: 'Maybe he went up over the roof and down the other side.'

The cop nodded: 'Yeah, might be. He sure acted funny — you'd thought he had something on his mind. When I called out to him he took off like a Flyin' Fortress and beat it up here — an' all I wanted to do was give him back this five-pound-note he dropped!'

She said: 'Why not keep the money? If he ran like you say he can't have needed it much.'

'Maybe you're right: but him running that way's made me kinda anxious to see him, see? Seems he had plenty to be frightened of. Guess I'll keep lookin' — over the roof.'

She snorted: 'Then you'd better get on with it instead of treating yourself to a free burlesque show, hadn't you, or he'll be miles away by the time you get to him!'

The cop grunted: 'Yeah — yeah — er

— so long, lady — er — I guess you wouldn't be doin' nothin' tonight, would you?'

She said: 'I'm not dated; no.'

'Then maybe you'd — er — like to have dinner an' a show?'

'I would,' she told him, then added: 'But not with *you*!'

There was silence again: Johnny heard the flat feet pounding up the escape. He came out of hiding and looked at the girl.

3

All Comers

She was out of the bath now and she had
on a filmy green robe, which just concealed enough of her youth and beauty to
make a man want to see the rest.

She was beautiful; there wasn't any
doubt of that. But Johnny had seen as
good-looking if not better, and he still
didn't care for women. He didn't know
that this one had something different, far
as he was concerned. Yet —

He looked at her, and she returned his
gaze with interest.

She said: 'And now suppose you give me
an explanation of why you were so anxious to dodge a policeman who only wanted
to give you a five-pound-note you'd lost?'

He grunted: 'Suppose you mind your
own business and find me the key to this
door! Or do I have to get tough again?'

The look she gave him would have

withered a more sensitive man. But there wasn't a sensitive nerve in Johnny's body.

'*No!*' she told him, point blank. 'I *asked* you a question . . .'

'What makes you figure I'll give you an answer?'

'You should. I was decent enough to front you out of a nasty jam — at least, you seemed to think it was a jam.'

He sneered: 'Decent enough? Lay off, sister! The only reason you fronted for me there was because you'd already been slapped down, and you didn't want no pistol blasting the hell outta your guts! That's what. Because you was scared silly . . .'

She gazed at him queerly. 'Of — *you?*'

'Of me! That smack kinda warned you I wasn't goin' to stand for no funny play . . .'

'You *did* hit me, didn't you? And you hurt, too! I owe you something for *that*. So perhaps if I square up now it'll convince you I didn't front for you because your gun, or you, worried me.'

And taking a forward step she swept her hand up and slapped him with all her force across the side of the face.

'Why, you — !' His gun came swiveling up. She stood there calmly, looking him in the eyes.

The gun dropped again and he rubbed his jaw.

'You mighta gotten yourself blasted to the pearly gates then, sister! Ain't you got any sense at all?'

'I might, mightn't I? You could easily have done it. You have a silenced automatic — I noticed that when you came in; and then by your own confession you're already a killer!'

'Then why *did* you do it?'

She smiled: '*Nobody* gets away with hitting me. And on top of that I wanted to show you I certainly wasn't afraid of *your kind*, and that I could have told that policeman about you being here, just as calmly as I hit you! Now do you *believe* you frightened me into helping you?'

He sat on the edge of the bath. He said: 'How do they call you?'

'My name's Stella Fraser. What's yours?'

'For now we'll skip that. What made you put up that play on my account, Stella?'

She hesitated, shrugged. Then said: 'I don't know; impulse maybe. And I — liked the way you looked.'

'How did I look?'

'Handsome — but very scared! I felt sorry for you.'

'Yeah. You're a funny kid, ain't you?'

'Am I? Why?'

'You always act on sudden hunches like you did then?'

'Often — always have. But — it wasn't entirely the hunch as you call it. It was mainly even vaguer than that. Just a feeling inside, a feeling that I was meant to cover up for you . . . I won't try to explain it anymore.'

He regarded her admiringly. He said: 'I kinda like you, kid. No dame's ever had the chance to slap me down before, and even given the chance they'd think twice before they did, and then they wouldn't, anyway. But you go right ahead — take your chance. Maybe you didn't know I got a temper like a wild horse?'

She shrugged: 'Didn't care.'

'A funny thing that I didn't plug you. I was hopping mad when you slugged me.

I don't know what held me back . . . something did. Maybe the same thing made you cover up for me.'

He got up and slid his gun back into his pocket. He said: 'I better blow now — '

'You still haven't told me just why you were running, and who you killed.'

'Nope, I ain't. Well, I was running because I figured the cop was on my tail, and I killed a dirty, lowdown, no-good, double-dealing rat, back in another city.'

'Is that *all* you're going to tell me?'

'I guess it is. Who I am doesn't matter right now. I'm just a bum on the run.'

'You say the man you killed was — no good?'

'You're quoting me there. None at all. He had to get it sooner or later, so why not sooner, and from me? He crossed me and the boys up . . . '

'Me and the boys? You — mean a — *gang*?'

'Somethin' of that description an' designation.'

She bent and forked down in the pockets of her costume. She came up with the key, said: 'Think you'll be safe to leave now?'

'What difference of yours is it?'

She shook her head: 'I'm interested in you, that's all. And after I've taken all the trouble I have to scare trouble away from you, I wouldn't want you running right out into it, now would I?'

He took the key, fitted it to the lock. He said: 'I have to take a chance. I always have to take a chance. What could you do to help?'

'I could let you stay a while.'

He paused: 'Here?'

'Why not?'

He laughed, looking closely at her. 'I don't get it — what makes you so darn keen to lend a lame dog a helpin' hand? You ain't the come-hither type by the look of you. You ain't the type that'd be interested in any dough I might have — or are you?'

'Are you *trying* to insult me?'

'Nope. Just trying to get you straight. Because if it's dough you want I got none.'

'I asked you if you'd care to stay here

until you fancy it'd be safe for you to leave. You haven't answered yet.'

He opened the door and walked through. He said: 'Okay, sister. I stay. Get your duds on an' we'll have a chat about this an' that.'

She closed the door, and he listened at the keyhole to make sure she wasn't leaning out of the window bawling for all kinds of coppers and detectives. She wasn't. She wasn't making a sound. He peeked through: she was getting into her slip. She wasn't even looking at the window. He went and sat down, found a small table with a few bottles of lager in a cupboard under it, opened and poured himself one.

He was drinking it and smoking when she came back. She was dressed in a powder-blue costume, the one he'd seen lying on the bathroom chair, and she was looking prettier than ever with her fair, wavy hair out of the bath net. She looked absurdly young to have any dealings with a crook, and to handle him as coolly as she had.

She smiled at him: 'Comfortable?'

'Hear me objectin'?'

'Maybe you're hungry?'

'Why? You got something on the boil?'

'Nothing in, but I can slip down to the delicatessen . . . '

He got up and his hand hovered near his gun pocket. He snarled: 'Sister, if I was within an inch of starvation I wouldn't trust you to go down and get eats alone, and have you bringin' half the flatties in London back here with you. Siddown.'

She tilted her dainty little nose.

'You're rather surly, aren't you?'

'I gotta be. The world don't play fair with guys in my profession, lady.'

'You'll have me crying in a minute, you poor man,' she sniffed. 'Do *you* play fair in the world?'

'Sure. I never shoot unless I either have to or I lose my temper. If I lose my temper easy and often that's the world's hard luck, but not my fault.'

She said: 'Wait a second . . . you look as if you're famished.'

She walked over to the door and he admired her slim legs and the golden tan of them. She opened the door, and he growled:

'Watch what you're doing . . . '

She called: 'Izzy — *oh*, Izzy!'

There was the sound of a door opening along the passage, then a kid's voice said: 'Yeah, Miss Fraser?'

'Will you run down to the deli for me, and bring two orders of ham and eggs and French fries, and anything else they have that looks nice. Bring a jug of coffee with a carton of cream — tell Moe I'll look after the jug for him. Here's sixpence for yourself, Izzy. And hurry.'

'Gee, thanks, Miss Fraser. I'll only be a few minutes!'

Izzy beat it down the stairs, and the girl came back into the room. She said, with a hint of scorn in her tone:

'Satisfied?'

Johnny nodded: 'I guess.'

'Sure I didn't tell Izzy what was wrong by slipping him a note?'

'I thought of that — but you haven't written any note.'

'I could have done whilst I was getting dressed in the bathroom, couldn't I?'

'Yeah — but I happen to know you didn't.'

'Mind reader?'

'Nothin' so clever. I was watchin' you through the keyhole!'

'You were?' She flushed a little. 'I see. A peeping Tom!'

'That's about it. And I have to admit you don't do so bad as a Lady Godiva yourself. Now, if you just had a horse — '

'We'll drop that subject.'

She went to the window and looked out. She said: 'You need a shave, don't you.'

'Kind of. I been travelling ever since I lammed out of . . . well, where I lammed out of. I ain't eaten and I ain't washed or shaved either.'

She jerked a thumb towards the bathroom. 'There's a cupboard in there. Inside there's a straight razor the last tenant left, and that I use for unpicking dresses and things. There's a strop with it — if you like you can go and wash and shave . . . '

He looked at her suspiciously. She smiled faintly, walked to the door, turned the key in the lock then gave it to him.

She said: 'Here, if you're still worried. Take the key — then I can't get out to bring help, can I?'

He took the key and went into the bathroom. He heard her singing, heard the rattle of crockery and cutlery. She was *setting a table for the food!*

He scraped at his stubble with the razor. It was the toughest shave he'd ever had, because there was only washing soap to use for lathering, and normally he was accustomed to an electric razor. But he got through at length, and started washing. Then he used a clothes brush to good effect on his pants and jacket, gave a twitch to his tie, adjusted his coat, and went back into the other room — to find the girl sitting beside the table with two places set and two large portions of ham and French fries.

She said: 'Through?'

'Sure. Feel better for it. Say, that looks like real grub.'

'It smells like it, too. Sit down here.'

He sat down and started eating; then stopped with fork halfway to mouth. He grunted: 'Listen — if that outer door was locked and I had the key, how come the kid got this stuff in to you?'

She threw another key on the table. She smiled: 'I had this key! I let you have the other so's you'd feel safe. But you don't really need to worry about me. I wouldn't give you away. Haven't you realized I don't mean to, yet?'

He stared at her curiously. He said: 'I'm beginning to . . . '

After that he didn't speak for some time, not until there was an empty plate in front of him, and a steaming cup of coffee in his hand.

* * *

The clock over the hearth struck seven. He stopped talking and lit a cigarette. She said: 'Well, you've heard my story, and now I've heard yours. Seems we've both had to hack our own way through in life.'

'Yeah. Except my hacking's been somewhat more gruesome than yours. And you still haven't explained why you're doing all this for me.'

'All what?'

'Letting me stay here, for instance.'

'For the same reason you're staying, I suppose it is. Why don't you go now?'

'I can't tell — I just don't want to go.'

'And I don't want to give you away. It isn't so strange as it seems. Funnier things *have* happened, you know.'

'Not to me they haven't.'

She said: 'Didn't you say you'd like to see the evening paper?'

'Sure. But how do I get to see it? You reckon you don't get one, don't you?'

'I don't. But there's a newsstand at the corner. I'll slip out and get you one if you like.'

He sat up and snapped: 'No.'

She studied him pityingly. 'You aren't still afraid I'll try something, are you?'

He took his time answering. When at last it came it indicated that there'd been an inward struggle. But she'd won! He grunted: 'Make it snappy, Stella.'

She got up and went out. While she was away he paced up and down the room. Had he been a fool to give her a chance to get the cops? Or had he? But — she could have beat it earlier if she'd wanted,

48

when he was in the bathroom. Why shouldn't he trust her?

Then again — suppose she did come back with a bunch of cops?

How about that?

He sat down abruptly; no, she wouldn't, he told himself. Not a chance. It wasn't in her eyes. He couldn't say what really *was* in her eyes, but it wasn't treachery.

As if to echo his thoughts the door opened and she came in and slapped three papers on the table.

'I got one of each. All right?'

He picked them up and went swiftly through them. There wasn't anything in the first two.

The other one gave a brief account of the trouble in Mugs Alley, and an even briefer description of the missing gang men. It seemed no one knew which of the gang had done the killing. Nor were there any pictures of any of them. Maybe that'd come later, but for now Johnny felt he was safe.

He told the girl: 'Like to step out?'

She nodded at once: 'I think so. Where could we go?'

'We'll see when we hit the drag. Get your glad rags on and let's go. Maybe there'll be a good movie on someplace.'

They got out and started pushing their way through the crowd along Sussex Street. They passed two cinemas, but the movies that were on there didn't seem too promising.

They sauntered on, Johnny involuntarily stiffening every time they passed a policeman. In between times he talked to Stella.

'Dough's what I need,' he told her. 'If I could just get my fingers on, say, a few hundred pounds — I could get a start in a new racket here.'

'But — how?'

'Easy. If you know the ropes it ain't hard to start in a small way, baby. Then you gradually work your way up . . . '

She smiled: 'It sounds good. But is it all *that* easy?'

'Easier. If I can just get my mitts on two, three hundred pounds, maybe I'll show you.'

He jerked to a halt suddenly outside a garishly painted and lighted building.

Almost reverently he breathed:

'Great Jumpin' Frankfurters! A gift from the Gods!'

She followed his gaze; the name on the ribbon banner above the hall read: 'Sussex Hall — All-in Wrestling Every Night with the Kings of the Mat.'

But the sign Johnny was staring at so rapturously was at the side, and said: 'The Cockney Maniac issues a challenge to all heavyweights, and members of the public. Unbeaten King of the Ring challenges anyone to make him kiss the mat with his shoulders. The Maniac will personally guarantee three hundred pounds to the man who can get him down and keep him down. The Maniac, direct from his championship win, has fought three hundred fights. He has yet to be beaten. No holds barred. The winner to be the man who is able to walk from the ring. Side stake of twenty pounds. Nothing to pay to challenge. All comers, age and weight of no account. The Cockney Maniac is appearing at this hall only tonight. He has already been challenged by two of the leading heavyweights here. I. Solway, the promoter, personally guarantees all fights taking place in this hall to be devoid of staging. Admission: Two-and-six; Five Shillings; Ten Shillings.'

Stella looked at him, and gasped: 'You don't mean — ?'

'Why not? I'm no sucker at the mat game. I used to tumble around in a fair booth until I got too important for small-time stuff like wrestling.'

'But — you aren't a heavyweight.'

'Says age an' weight don't count. So what's to stop me steppin' in an' cleaning up?'

'But you'll be — *hurt* . . . You couldn't stand up to a man like this Maniac must be. Don't do it, please.'

He smiled grimly; said: 'It says 'No Holds Barred.' Get it?'

4

On the Mat

'Laydees an' gennelmen,' bellowed the announcer into the ring mike. 'Tonight's programme consists of two heavyweight bouts between the Cockney Maniac, the greatest wrestling sensation of the age, and two of your own favourite mat-crawlers who have accepted his challenge . . . When the Maniac has disposed of these two boys — if he manages it — he will then issue an open challenge to any member of the general public! For a stake of three hundred pounds, which the Maniac and his promoter have guaranteed!

'Laydees an' gennelmen, the first bout of the evenin' is due on in five minutes.'

There was a buzz of whispering, and Johnny turned to Stella:

'All I can say is I hope one of the big lugs that've challenged him don't finish him off before I get to him . . . '

She shook her head; she was watching the ring anxiously.

There was a roar from the crowd where they lined the entrance tunnel from the dressing rooms.

'Yah! Dirty Huggins! Beat it, Huggins!'

Several Cockney cheers floated into the air, and the roaring swelled as the wrestler came into view. Apparently he was by no means a firm favorite.

There was another roar from the opposite side indicating the appearance of the Maniac.

Huggins climbed into the ring, discarded his dressing gown, and stood limbering up on the ropes.

He was a mountain of fat; fat flowed from him at all angles. His massive chest hung in wobbling folds over his belly, his legs resembled young trees. His hair was thinning on top of his bullet-shaped head. He wore short black trunks, and somewhat worn shoes.

Then the Maniac was climbing into the ring.

Stella gave a gasp, and Johnny looked a bit uncertain.

The Cockney Maniac stood about seven feet tall. The muscles on his arms and back put the village blacksmith to shame. His legs were hairy and strong, his hands like young hams. His hair was wild and disordered, and it was easy to see from his battered features and wild eyes where he'd got the name of Maniac from.

He lived up to the name, too; he snarled and foamed at the wrestler in the other corner, and made breaking motions with his hands. He jumped in the air with both feet and howled.

The crowd howled with him; this was what they'd come for.

This was what they loved!

The announcer came into the ring again, drew down the mike.

'Laydees an' gennelmen, this is a challenge fight, no rounds, no holds barred, between — on my right, the challenger — 'Orrible 'Uggins of Liverpool — '

'Send him out! Yah — get out, Huggins!'

'And introducing, on my left, none other than the famous Cockney Maniac!'

'Brrrrrr! Get outta it, ya nut!' bellowed

the supporters of Horrible Huggins.

The announcer went on: 'The referee — Bill Former!'

'Boooooo — why don' ya get a proper ref?'

The ref smiled sheepishly and motioned the two wrestlers to the centre of the ring. They stood, hands on hips, whilst he spoke briskly to them. They nodded. Huggins held out his hand. The Maniac spat in it. They went to their corners.

The bell went.

The Maniac came from his corner with a sideways movement. He circled away from Huggins. Huggins, wobbling like an immense jelly, spat: 'Git in an' fight, you yeller slob!'

The crowd bawled: 'Quit dancin', Maniac! What you want, some music? Get into him, ya dope!'

Huggins rushed in suddenly and got a grip on the Maniac's hands. They strained — then the Maniac lifted his foot and gave Huggins a kick that almost knocked his guts through his mouth. Huggins yelped: '*Aaaaah!*' then started squirming on the floor, the breath knocked out of him.

The Maniac jumped into the air, growling, came down with his muscular rear on Huggins's face. Huggins sank his teeth into the Maniac's posterior.

The Maniac came to his feet as if he'd sat on a hot stove.

He fairly gibbered with rage. He beat his chest and tore his hair. He kicked the recumbent Huggins in the teeth. Huggins tried to crawl away; the Maniac went after him, grabbed his scanty hair, hauled him upright. He drew his fist back and let Huggins have a sizzling roundhouse swing. Huggins shot back against the ropes.

The Maniac picked him up, gave him the aeroplane spin, threw him against the corner post. The now senseless Huggins flopped to the floor. The Maniac picked him up, as one of the seconds slung in the towel. He tossed him over the ropes on top of his two seconds.

Two ambulance men came with a stretcher and carried Huggins out. The crowd screeched.

The ref said to the Maniac: 'Hey, lengthen 'em out a bit, Cockney. The crowd want a show, bud.'

The Maniac fisted him in the teeth, and snarled: 'Who's fightin', you or me?'

The announcer climbed into the ring.

'Horrible Huggins having retired, the winner is the Cockney Maniac!'

The crowd settled down for the next bout. The announcer went on: 'The second challenger on this evening's programme is the Bearded Hill Billy, Australia.'

The Bearded Hill Billy had climbed into the ring and stood bowing to his audience. The Bearded Hill Billy, it seemed, was by way of being a blue-eyed boy with the fight fans. They yelled:

'Atta boy, Billy. Give him the Bear Hug, feller! You can't go wrong — give it to him!'

The Hill Billy grinned. He was a strapping figure of a man. And young: his luxurious whiskers were a fiery red. His back and chest were covered with hair as with a garment. He wore tights.

He went to the centre of the ring. The ref ran his hand down their arms and bodies, ordered the Hill Billy to remove a rough bandage from his wrist. He examined their shoes, said: 'There ain't any great hurry, boys. Put up a fair show . . .'

They got back to their corners.

The bell went; they came out. Seemingly it was a habit with the Australian to shake hands at the commencement of the round, before starting in earnest. He stuck his hand out. The Maniac repeated his stock gag of spitting into it. The Hill Billy character slapped it back into the Maniac's eyes, then, whilst the Maniac was temporarily blinded through wiping it off, the Hill Billy punched him in the stomach.

The Maniac went down, then bounced up again like a rubber ball. He said: '*Grrrrr!*'

He backed towards his corner; the Australian came after him. The Maniac went down on his knees, raised his hands in supplication. The spectators howled: 'Get him Billy!' and 'Watch him — he's foxin'!'

The Maniac, it seemed, was foxing. For his right hand suddenly went streaking back of him. When it came forward again it was holding the tin bucket from the corner. The Maniac got up, and as the Australian came in, slammed the bucket forcibly over the challenger's head, then swung the handle.

The Australian roared, his voice sounding enormous inside the tin bucket. The ref tried to help him get it off. The Maniac kicked the ref in the slats. The crowd roared: 'Send him out! Dirty Maniac!'

The ref was down with the Maniac on top of him, and the bucketed Hill Billy on top of them both. The Maniac had the ref's throat and was squeezing. The crowd yelled: 'Liven up, Former! He'll kill you! Haw, haw, haw!'

The Hill Billy had dislodged the bucket. He had got to his feet. He became aware of the Maniac still busy with the ref. He bent forward and dealt his adversary a terrific rabbit punch back of the neck. The Maniac flopped forward.

The Hill Billy grabbed his legs and dragged him clear of the ref. He pulled the legs upwards through his own, bent the Maniac backwards until the Maniac's back was in danger of snapping. The crowd shrieked: 'You got him, Billy! He'll have to submit!'

They spoke too soon. The Maniac could take it. He screamed with pain, but he held on. He didn't give a submission fall. It would have meant he'd lost the fight.

It was the first time the crowd had seen anyone defy that particular hold, known as the 'Boston Crab.' Too much of it could snap a man's back like a rotten twig. But the Maniac held on, and more, he made a supreme effort, twisted half over, grabbed the Hill boy's legs, and hauled.

The Australian came down with a thud that rang through the building. The Maniac lay panting and squirming. He crawled to the ropes, hauled his aching body to its feet.

The Australian was coming in again; the Maniac feigned semi-consciousness. The Hill Billy was neatly tricked into making an injudicious lunge with his head.

The Maniac moved swiftly aside, and the Australian went half out of the ring. The Maniac speeded him on with a timely kick in the shorts.

The challenger picked himself up and

climbed back to the ringside. The Maniac bent out and grabbed his hair, pulled him in a somersault into the ring. Before the Hill Billy knew what was what his neck was again through the ropes, and two strands were twisted about it, choking him, cutting off his breathing. The ref was in play again, trying to untwist the ropes. The Maniac took a flying leap, landed with his feet on the Hill Billy's spine.

The ref had released the Hill Billy, who staggered dazedly back to the centre of the ring. There were wild cries of: 'Look out, Billy — wake up, ya nut — '

The Maniac, grinning savagely, fetched up his left foot under the Australian. The Hill boy groaned and pitched forward on his face. The Maniac grabbed his arm, started to twist it behind his back.

He twisted, not wisely, but too well. The Hill Billy suddenly gave a loud shriek and started squirming all over the ring. His left arm dangled limply. The seconds tossed in the towel.

The ref rushed over and dragged the Maniac off. He said: 'Lay off — you've done it. Dislocation.'

The Maniac cooled down; he pointed to the Hill Billy's flailing arm and legs. The seconds and the ref grabbed and held them. The beaten challenger roared in agony, as the Maniac took a firm grip of his dislocated arm, pulled, jerked — and the arm slid into place at the shoulder socket again.

The crowd bawled themselves hoarse again. They loved anything like that. The announcer got up and held up the Maniac's arm. They carried the dilapidated Hill Billy from the ring. He was able to walk to his dressing room, and the crowd gave him a rousing cheer.

Stella was shuddering, feeling faint and sick. Johnny wasn't looking any too bright either. He had a feeling that even his neat rough-housing tricks couldn't save him from mayhem if he got into that ring.

The announcer announced: 'Laydees an' gennelmen — before we get on to the rest of the events on this programme, the Maniac issues a challenge to anyone wishing to meet him, here and now.'

He was smiling; after the display that had happened there wasn't anyone in that audience who'd pit themselves against the Maniac. There never was — the Maniac was a killer, not a rassler!

But tonight he was wrong. Two men came to their feet.

A big, beefy-looking man with red features and bulging muscles; and a tall, dark, muscular man at the ringside.

The announcer gaped, and the Maniac showed his teeth. The audience yelled with anticipation.

The two climbed into the ring. The announcer took the burly man first: 'You wish to — to *challenge* the Maniac?'

'Sure thing. Why you figure I'm here if not?'

'Where you from?'

'Middlesbrough. I'm a steel worker. Name of Hammerton.'

The announcer grunted. 'It's your funeral, pal. Go back to the dressing room and get rigged up with pants and shoes. Then get back here.'

Hammerton went. The announcer turned to the other man: 'How about you, mister?'

'Just announce me as a guy from

Liverpool. Independent.'

'Ain't you a touch light to rassle the Maniac? You'd be givin' him about four stone.'

'That's my affair. Your bill out there says age and weight ain't important.'

'Okay, son, we'll send you flowers. Head back with that other sap and get rigged up. You'll follow him . . . '

Johnny climbed from the ring; Stella was white, clutching her handkerchief nervously. She'd begged him not to mix with the Maniac, but Johnny had been set. He'd said he would, and he wasn't going to back out front of any dame now. Not Johnny. Whatever else he lacked he didn't lack guts — but he might, when the Maniac was through with him, he reflected grimly.

The announcer caught the air again as the steel worker stepped into the ring. The man wasn't looking any too happy about it, but he wasn't backing out. The announcer wondered how these mugs hoped to beat the Maniac when professional rasslers couldn't!

He said: 'Laydees an' gennelman! The

Maniac's challenge has been accepted by the man on the right — Fightin' Tommy Hammerton of Middlesbrough. No holds barred, no liability to management of this emporium.'

He got out of the ring; the bell went.

The Maniac came from his corner curiously, took a good long look at the steel worker, who was plenty muscular under his clothes.

The steel worker looked unhappy. The fans cued: 'Come on, Middlesbrough! Use him like you would a steel girder.'

'Sure, smoke him out, pal.'

Spurred on to doughty deeds by this encouragement, the challenger dashed hazily across towards the Maniac, swinging his arms like windmill sails.

The Maniac stuck an interested fist in his path. Middlesbrough took it on the nose, fell back, yelling.

The Maniac kicked him casually in the stomach and watched him flop onto the ropes. Middlesbrough came groggily to his feet and the Maniac grabbed a fistful of the hair growing on his chest and threw him over the ring by it.

Then he was taken by the neck as if he were a child, his head was tucked beneath the Maniac's arm, and he was rushed over the ring at terrific speed, to the corner pad.

Whump!

That *was* Hammerton's head meeting the pad.

Thud!

That was Hammerton's pant's seat meeting the boards.

The Maniac advanced viciously. He was getting into his stride.

Hammerton blinked dazedly up, yelped, scrabbled to the ropes, slid under them, and still half dazed raced up the tunnel to the dressing rooms.

Handling steel girders was one thing — handling a guy like the Cockney Maniac was another. Middlesbrough didn't wonder he hadn't been defeated yet.

The crowd jeered, laughed — then quietened as Johnny stepped into the ring.

5

Johnny Pulls It Off

Whilst the announcer was going through the preliminary introductions, Johnny weighed the Maniac up.

The Maniac was tiring; four bouts one after the other might prove too much for him, Johnny considered. Of course two of the bouts had been mere routs, but the fight with the Australian had without doubt taken it out of the Cockney wrestler.

The Maniac, in his corner, had little doubt of his ability to massacre this younger man in double quick time.

Johnny was muscular and tall; but the Maniac was muscular and even taller.

Johnny wanted to win three hundred pounds — but the Maniac didn't want to lose three hundred pounds! Both had good reasons for being grimly determined.

The Maniac wasn't worrying though, if Johnny was. He was a pro, and well able to deal with any amateur who stepped into the ring. He wasn't aware that his challenger had wrestling experience at his own weight, and he was even less aware of the rough-housing Johnny had done in his time. He felt he would be able to handle the tall young man as easily as if he were a baby.

He had noticed where Johnny had been sitting, mainly on account of the girl with him. The Maniac was a sucker for women. Now he leaned over his corner towards her, called: 'Lady, when they've took your guy to the morgue maybe you'll let a real man take you home, huh?'

He didn't get any answer. Stella's face was quite pale.

She felt Johnny hadn't a chance against such a brute as the Maniac.

But two things were going to help Johnny through: one of them alone might not have helped much. But combined they added up to a rough passage for the Maniac. The first of them was there all the time — it was determination.

The second was to come later.

The ref beckoned them into the centre of the ring and spieled something to the Maniac about 'taking it easy with the kid.'

They went back to the corners without shaking. Johnny thought too much of his hand to let the Maniac have the chance of spitting in it.

The bell went!

Johnny came out warily. He knew that if he let the Maniac get a decent hold on him he was sunk. What he had to do was keep on circling, waiting until he could get a few kidney punches home to slow the Maniac down.

But the Maniac was getting tired. He felt he'd given the customers a run for their dough, and he wanted to get out. Furthermore, the announcer had suggested to him that he might as well speed things up — there were still two minor bouts to be fought, and time was wasting.

Therefore he didn't waste any time in circling and looking for a good point of attack. He rushed — and unprepared for the suddenness of it, Johnny was taken by surprise and before he knew just how things were going he was battered forcibly backwards on to the canvas, every ounce of breath knocked from his body. The Maniac got a leg lock and hauled. Then squirming round until Johnny was in position for stretching. He stretched; Johnny groaned.

Stella, at the ringside, half came from her seat with a cry.

The Maniac hammered a knobby fist into Johnny's spine, and Johnny flopped forward with a hoarse croak.

Then the Maniac became overconfident. He did something which was very unfortunate, from his point of view. He decided to give the crowd a final laugh, and accordingly turned Johnny over his knee.

Face downwards.

Then with a heavy hand he commenced to paddle the seat of his shorts!

He said: 'An' if this don't teach you to respec' your elders mebby I'll keep you in after school! Har, har!'

The crowd laughed like a bunch of hyenas. 'Haw, haw, haw!'

And Johnny suddenly realized what a

fool he was looking and snapped out of the semidaze he'd been in!

His temper snapped entirely. It was the second thing which was to help him through. Coupled with his previous determination he now became a formidable opponent even to the Maniac.

There wasn't anything the Maniac could have done which would have so roused Johnny's temper as that paddling stunt did.

The Maniac wasn't ready for the sideways twist Johnny gave. He wasn't ready for the sudden recovery. He'd meant to give Johnny a few more wallops then sling him out. But it didn't work out like that.

Johnny rolled from his knee, rolled half way across the ring. He came to his feet quickly, his face livid. He said: 'You bastard!'

The Maniac got up from his knees. Here was this young runt still in the game when he thought he had him.

He came for Johnny; and Johnny altered his tactics. He threw himself backwards against the ropes, using them as a catapult, and launched himself with unbelievable velocity at the Maniac's belly. He hit fair and square. The Maniac simply coiled up like a jackknife with a low gurgling noise.

Johnny got off the floor, threw himself at the other ropes, shot off again, took the crouching Maniac smack in the small of the back. The Maniac went down.

Johnny piled on, hauled *his* legs backwards.

The crowd roared — the Maniac was in the Boston Crab lock for the second time that night — and Johnny put it on viciously, bending the Maniac almost in two, coming within an ace of snapping the wrestler's spine.

There was a sudden roaring from the Maniac, and an agonized hammering at the canvas. The ref tapped Johnny on the shoulder.

'He submits! Drop him — drop him, you fool!'

Because Johnny was going on bending, and the Maniac was shrieking.

Slowly it percolated through. Johnny let the Maniac's legs flop down. The Maniac lay where he'd been dropped, unable to move.

The seconds climbed in, gave him a once over. Johnny said: 'He all right?'

'Sure. You nearly fixed him forever though, son. That's the worst of you amateurs who don't know the game. You don't know when to stop.'

'I'm no amateur, mister. Used to wrestle for a living back in Liverpool. The guy just got my goat, that's all. He don't want to go making dopes outta fellers.'

The announcer was saying: 'Ladees an' gennelmen, the Cockney Maniac, having submitted to a Boston Crab, the winner is the — ah hell, the unknown young man from Liverpool!'

The crowd cheered themselves wild.

The announcer handed something to the Maniac who was now almost recovered after a vigorous back massage. He hobbled to the centre of the ring. He shook hands with Johnny. He said: 'Good fight, kid. If you ever feel like takin' wrestlin' up for keeps get in touch with me. Here's your dough . . . I hate to give it ya, but ya earned it!'

Johnny took it. He could hardly believe he'd won. But three hundred pounds . . . and a side stake of fifty — enough to get a fresh start.

Tomorrow! No time like the present . . . and maybe he could use Stella to help him. She seemed to have brought him luck!

★　　★　　★

Johnny said: 'You got any scruples kid?'

'That depends — morally, you mean?'

'Nope, not that way. Business scruples — I mean do you care much how you make dough, long as you make it?'

She reflected: 'I don't know — I haven't ever thought of it. I wouldn't mind doing something shady — long as it wasn't too bad. I think almost everyone has stolen in their time, even if it's only been a trifle. Why, Johnny?'

He told her: 'I figure I might be able to use you in the racket I'm going into.'

'What is it, Johnny? I couldn't give you a great deal of time. I have a job as a stenographer you know.'

'The hell with your job. We'll make plenty on this — first of all, how about it?'

'If it isn't *too* bad I'll come in with you, Johnny.'

'Then I'll give you the lowdown on it. First off we hire an office here, see. A cheap office, an' we give out false names. We then insert an ad in the popular magazines, the pulp papers. An ad that runs:

'Sex Customs Throughout the World! The Bandero Publishing Co., Ltd., of London, offer you an amazing new book by a world famed traveller. Details of the startling sex practices of Hindu, Chinese, Russian, American, English. True life photographs showing in intimate detail, step by step sequences of exotic parties in the artists' quarters of Paris, Chelsea and Greenwich Village.

'Unbelievably erotic Geisha girls, strange marriage customs of little known African tribes. Women of every race and creed feature in this new book by the Bandero Publishing Co. Rush order. Supplies strictly limited.

'Five shilling edition, bound in stiff

boards on fine art paper.

'Deluxe edition in heavy red cloth with gilt lettering on back and spine, seven and sixpence.

'Sent to you under plain cover a few days after receipt of order. No C.O.D. No orders. Send cash with form below and delivery will take place within seven days.'

He looked at her; he said: 'See? That's how I'll word it. I'll take as much space as three hundred pounds can buy in the national mags, and run the ad. I've had some experience of the British public. They're suckers, a nation of them, for patent medicines, horoscopes, uplift bras, in fact, anything that can be had through mail-order. They'll buy blindly, taking a chance. If they get stung that's their fault. Furthermore, an ad like the one I've mentioned appeals to thousands.

'They collect books like that. Revel in 'em. Old roués. Get it?'

'There's just one thing I don't get, Johnny. If you plan to spend three hundred an ad space, and fifty on an office payment, how do you get the money to print the book?'

He said, blandly: 'What book?'

She gaped: 'The one you — you plan to advertise?'

'There ain't any book, sugar. Listen — the money'll come rolling in for a week after that ad gets printed. We'll cash in good. For seven days. Then we fold our tents like the Arabs and as silently steal away. See?'

'But how about the books? All those people . . . '

'Suckers. An' if they send dough to buy a book like that they ask for all they get.'

'Do you mean — you mean just walk off with their money?'

'Surest thing. Vamoose pronto. Quite amazin' the way we'll disappear. We'll be gone long before the suckers start getting excited about their orders.'

'But — the police?'

'Won't find us. And very few of the suckers'll bother the cops about it. Would you, if you'd sent off for a filthy book an' been dished? Would you go an' tell it all to the cops? They'd say you'd got what you asked for, anyway.'

She seemed startled; said: 'And you think they'll fall for it? Send their money on the strength of an ad?'

'You'd be surprised, kid. Besides, how are they to know they're stepping into a fast con game? There's dozens of mail-order firms who do business this way — thousands in fact. The majority, say ninety-five percent, are dead genuine. It's only the odd one here an' there that's playin' some kind of a trick. The public'll send off their dough just as trustingly as they send it to any of the other firms. See?'

'But you might be cheating them out of their last penny!'

'If they'll spend their last penny on an ad like that they deserve to be cheated out of it.'

'And when you've got the money . . . ?'

'Start a better racket with it. Work on up. And you'll be right along. Now, how's about it, Stella? Play ball?'

She looked at him steadily for a minute. There seemed to be a struggle inside of her as she strove to reconcile herself to making crooked money — with him! And because she felt more than ever that they were meant to stick together, she at last said: 'I'll do all you want of me, Johnny. I'm with you!'

★ ★ ★

They found an office in a cheap district, and weren't asked too many questions. It was small and shabby and its furniture consisted of a battered desk and one waste basket. It was cheap and it was ideal for their purpose.

They moved in right the next day and Johnny drafted out the ad for the mags. He sent it off the same night, and knew it would be published within a couple of days, in eight popular magazines.

This was a racket of his own. Mail-order crooks were common enough, but not in this department. Most of the book ads were quite genuine. And he knew how much appeal the type of book explained in his ad held for the average citizen. Esoteric writing was always a big draw, never failed. Mail-order firms published an edition of anywhere from one to two hundred thousand copies when they had something sure selling.

They sat back and waited then. They were still living in her rooms. He slept in the sitting room, she in her bedroom. She had principles, and as yet there wasn't anything wrong between them. But they'd fallen together like the King and Queen of Hearts, and they stayed that way.

If she was doing something which before had seemed terribly wrong, she dismissed it from her mind. She only knew she wanted to stay with Johnny, and if staying with Johnny meant she had to live according to his lights, then that she was prepared to do.

Three days passed, and during the three days they spent some time seeing the town. Johnny spent her money freely, and she didn't object. To her he had become a kind of hero — she felt that if he had done anything wrong, it couldn't have been his fault. She admired his nerve and strength, had fallen for him really big ever since he had stepped up against the Maniac.

The third day brought a flood of mail. It almost swamped the tiny office.

Some of the would-be buyers of the

81

book had ordered C.O.D. Some had sent cheques. The cheques Johnny destroyed. They would be a sure give-away.

They spent all of that day opening letters and banding money into neat piles. Barnum had once claimed there was a sucker born every minute — right now it seemed the rate must have speeded up, and there must be one born every half second.

At the end of the day they checked up on the money which had been strapped into hundred-pound wads.

Johnny said: 'Holy lice, this is even more than I figured on. Five thousand quid!'

She was worried: 'It's ever such a lot, Johnny. Are you sure it's safe?'

'Sure it is,' he said reassuringly. 'I used to work this racket when I was nineteen. But it don't do to play it too long — if you keep on at it sooner or later they get you. We won't play it too long, though, see. We'll slide out fast soon as the seven days are up, and leave the suckers to squawk!'

The next day's mail was even heavier.

The caretaker of the block of offices looked at them in surprise, said: 'They left a special mail bag for you down in my office.'

Johnny went to get it, brought it up. Thousands of letters fell out on the floor. From people of all types and descriptions, some of whom had written an enclosure note. They came from miners, from bankers, from farm hands, from mannequins, from film idols, from burlesque dolls, from chimney cleaners and ice-men, from fruit hawkers, and cops, from school teachers and navy boys.

Spinsters, bachelors, married men and women, adolescents, even kids of ten and twelve (judging by the handwriting on some of the letters).

That day found them another seven thousand in hand.

And so it went on, the day after, and the day after that.

Until on the seventh day Johnny counted up and found that their assets now totaled, in pound notes, well over twenty thousand pounds!

From all over the country they had

come, from Scotland to Kent, from Wales to Hull.

And that night they threw the opened envelopes into a tray at one side of the office, removed all trace of their possession, and hightailed it out of the district, carrying a large bag containing twenty-three thousand pounds!

6

Twenty-Five Per

They moved out of Stella's apartments and into a swell flat in Mayfair. The next few days Stella sweated and stayed in, half afraid. Johnny didn't display any such emotion. He was busy on his next step upwards. This was more difficult.

First of all he contacted the firm that had used to supply him with pin tables back in Liverpool. They were a Midland firm, and he gave a false name, the one of Johnny Carter, which he had adopted for all practical purposes these days.

'This is John Carter,' he told the trade manager when he got through. 'I'm thinking of going into the pin table business in a big way. I wondered if you could supply me with about three hundred machines . . . ?'

'We can do that. But we must insist on cash.'

'Cash it'll be. What terms?'

'We can let you have a hundred of grade A models, K10 style, assorted designs, 10 balls a penny type with tilt device for fifty pounds each. A hundred assorted fruit machines, stock exchange type, for thirty-five pounds each, and the other hundred mixed at various prices from seventy pounds to one hundred and twenty.'

'How about quantity discount?'

'Ten percent, on every hundred,' he told him.

Johnny said: 'Okay. Send 'em to the goods yard, main depot. I'll pick 'em up from there. I'll forward a cheque the minute you let me have the bill.'

He hung up. That was that.

Now he'd landed himself with three hundred machines. All he now needed was the joints to park them in.

He managed to buy up an old bowling alley on Elm Street that would serve fine. He could keep the bowling games running and install a hundred of his machines round the sides.

Then he got hold of a cheap but big room, in a fair state of preservation. He converted it, with the aid of four work-men, into a soda parlor. That was ostensibly its purpose, but actually it was to serve as a dump for another hundred of his machines. He had to have some blind like the bowl-ing alley or the soda parlor, for the cops frowned on pin saloons which were straight gambling haunts.

That saw two hundred of the machines off his hands.

Next he toured the soda fountains, the odd shops, the hop-halls, the tawdry movie palace lounges in Soho. He found most were supplied with pin tables. They were supplied by a guy called Elmer Corvet, it seemed, and Corvet had monopolies of the concessions in that district.

'How much is Corvet allowing you?' Johnny wanted to know.

'Twenty percent of takings,' they told him. He walked over to one of their machines. It was worn and sometimes it wasn't operating right. He slicked in a coin and tried it.

Then he sneered: 'It's a wonder you get any players on these! How long you had them?'

They considered, said: 'Three years, thereabouts.'

He nodded: 'I figured so. Well, if you tell Corvet to take his junk to hell out of your stores, and do your dealing with me, here's what you get: first off, twenty-five percent of profits. Second, a change of machines every six months. Third, a bonus on every hundred pounds I take.'

'Corvet'll be wild,' they had said, but most of them had jumped at the offer. Corvet's trouble was that he hadn't any competition. He didn't bother what state his machines were in. Nobody had tried to crab his business — until now.

Johnny crabbed it all right. Before a day was out he had his final hundred machines placed.

Now he needed boys, boys he could trust, who knew the pinball racket inside out. He needed collectors, mechanics, and general strong arms. He wasn't fool enough to kid himself. Corvet wasn't going to take things lying down; he decided his most likely bet would be to see Corvet himself.

Accordingly he got the address from a saloon proprietor, and went over there.

Corvet had a suite of rooms near his own new place. Corvet was talking to a number of tough characters when he arrived, and they were so heated they didn't notice the door opening back of them. Johnny stood silently in the room and listened to Corvet saying:

'But who is it, that's what I wanna know. What jerk's hippin' in on my territory? It ain't one o' the other big pins — we got an agreement that this acreage is mine, an' they're stickin' to that. I've been rung up by five more saloon men today — they're all asking me to take my tables outa their joints on account of they're starting dealing with a new man. Who? An' furthermore, I do hear tell some lug's bought the old Golden Globe Alley and set up pin games round the joint, and bought the Grubel Hall and converted it into a pin saloon plus soda fountain.'

One of the boys said: 'So what you aim to do, Elmer?'

Corvet shook his head: 'Ain't anything I can do. If I start busting up the joints where they're turning down my business,

I'll have the cops onto me in no time. You know that. The days when a guy could go round making his own rules an' regulations is gone. The cops don't like pin games, anyway; it'd only need an outbreak of wrecking to get me chased outta town. I'm boggled!'

Johnny pushed his way through. They all turned and stared at him. He came and stood in front of Corvet. He grinned: 'Hi, Elmer!'

Corvet was big and fat, so fat he resembled the mountain that wouldn't come to Mahomet. His brows were thick and black and his hands were covered at the backs with a thick layer of hair. His face might have belonged to a semi-imbecilic member of some anthropoid family.

But for all his sloping forehead he wasn't any dope.

He said: 'Who're you?'

Johnny said: 'The name's Carter — John Carter.'

'Yeah? An' what you want? This is a private discussion, bud!'

'I figured you might want to see me bad.'

'About what?'

'About the pin table game. I'm the monkey who's driving you to bankruptcy!'

One of the mugs came out with his rod. Corvet said: 'Drop it, Beelzebub. Maybe we ought to talk to the boy. What exactly brings you here, mister?'

Johnny said: 'I got a proposition for you. You can take it or toss it aside, I don't worry. It's the only way you'll come out of this shemozzle with your shirt round your neck.'

Corvet grunted: 'What's your spiel, mister?'

'Simple enough. I got the pin games and I got the places to put 'em. I also got two first-rate halls which'll clean up on them. You got a few broken-down machines and hardly any custom now. Like you said there ain't anything you can do but take it. You've been sitting pretty, letting the pounds clink in. You didn't expect competition, and you weren't ready for it. Now you got it you don't know what to do . . . ten years back you'd have gone round with your boys busting up the joints that told you to shift your pin tables out of it.

Maybe also you'd've busted up me. But right now things have altered — you can't get away with mayhem an' murder no more, Corvet.

'Okay. Here's my proposition: I got the machines and the halls — you got a bunch of good boys. I'm willin' to let you come in with me — fifty-fifty. I use your boys and we work together. I donate the new machines as my share of the bargain — you donate the use of your hall attendants, your mechanics, your collectors, and your gorillas.

'We split two ways after the boys've been paid. That's my deal. You can take it or leave it. If you don't want it I guess I won't have much trouble finding my own mob.'

Corvet stared at him for minutes. Then said: 'You got one hell of a nerve bustin' in my own rooms and propositioning me for the use of *my* boys.'

The man he'd called Beelzebub said: 'Take him on it, Elmer. It's all you can do.'

Corvet nodded slowly. 'Suppose I say yes, mister?'

'Then we'll get together and have a

long talk about it all.'

'Where you from?'

'That's my business. I don't aim to answer any questions, so you'll do as well not to ask them.'

Corvet said: 'Okay, if you're placed that way.'

Johnny went on: 'There's one other thing, Corvet — I've got a mighty ugly temper. When I get mad I get good and mad. If you try to cross me — or any of you boys try to cross me — ' he went on eyeing them grimly. 'I got a rod that'll do my talking for me!'

Corvet grunted: 'Don't get worried, Mister Carter. We won't do you any dirt, will we boys?'

The boys contributed a grunt, a surly grunt.

Corvet said: 'There y'are. The boys are all for it.'

Johnny said: 'Okay. I'll blow now — I'll call you later and we can arrange to meet when there ain't so many ears around. I got plans for extendin' our territory.'

He walked to the door; turned there. He said: 'I got swell plans, Corvet.

Wouldn't want *any* of 'em to go wrong — you get me?'

'Couldn't miss you,' Corvet said in an oily voice.

Johnny went out.

Corvet sat watching the door with a strange smile. He said nothing to anybody for some minutes. Then he murmured: 'Now there's a cocksure young feller, boys, eh? Plenty of go about him, huh?'

Someone snarled: 'Why don't you let us fix him?'

'Not so fast, boys, not so fast,' Corvet grinned. 'That young man has talent — he also has new machines, and our customers. So for the present he can go ahead — we'll welcome him with open arms. Fawn on him —

'Let him get the expandin' he's talkin' about done, and then one night, when he's walkin' home in the shadows, maybe Beelzebub will be walkin' along behind him — an' you know what Beelzebub is when it comes to using a gun effectively. Isn't that true, Beelzy?'

Beelzebub grinned: 'Mean we'll bump him, boss?'

'What else? But not until after he's done everything he can to assist us. Let him give the pin table racket new life — let him use as much of his own money as he likes to brisk it up. Then we'll step in as his partners and claim his tables and his hall — after we've given him a one-way ticket for the river Styx. Get it, boys?'

When the boys left him later he was still smiling.

★　★　★

Johnny phoned Corvet towards evening, said: 'I have to talk with you. Where can we meet?'

'I usually eat at the Silver Bowl when I'm eatin' out,' Corvet told him. 'But maybe you'd want somewhere more private?'

'Maybe so. You know anywhere?'

'There's a spot over on Clifton Street. It's a Greek restaurant run by a Chinaman, Olly Lee. Buddy of mine — he'll fix us up in a private room — an' say, Carter — '

'Yeah?'

'I'll have a dame along — '

'Okay, Corvet. If you ring him, say to make it dinner for four. I may have company myself.'

Corvet said: 'Olly Lee's on Clifton Street, is where you want. The name of the eatery is the Athenia. About seven?'

'About that.' Johnny hung up. He turned to Stella who'd been listening to the monologue from his end. He said: 'We're dinin' tonight, baby. With one of the gang big wigs from this burg. Put on your best bib an' tucker lady, and look lovely.'

'Oh, but Johnny, I don't want to come. I'd feel out of place.'

'Nuts. Corvet's bringing his dame — so I want you along. You'll put 'em all to shame, kid.'

'But, Johnny, I don't like the idea . . . '

'Rubbish. Sooner or later you'll have to meet our new partner. It might as well be right now.'

She said: 'I'm worried, Johnny. I'm dead worried. Are you sure this Corvet is to be trusted?'

Johnny grinned: 'I don't trust him no further than I could trust a sailor with a showgirl in a dark alley. But he's goin' to be very useful, sugar. I need his help, an' I need the help of his boys. I figure it won't be so hard to alienate his mob. They don't love him any from what I seen of them. I'll work round 'em until they don't much care what happens to that fat slob. Then — whooooosh!'

'Johnny! What do you mean — *whooooosh*?' she gasped.

'Bang, bang,' he grinned, in a high good humour.

'You mean you'll — *shoot* him? Oh, Johnny, no!'

'Why not? That's what he plans to have done to me later.'

'You only suspect that . . . '

'I *know* that! I'm no dope, baby. After I left the room I lent an ear at the keyhole. I heard just what he planned to do to me. An' it was just what I planned to do to him!'

She looked worried: 'But suppose he does it first?'

Johnny looked grim for a minute. His

hands tightened.

He said: 'Don't worry. He won't!'

*　　*　　*

She dressed carefully that night, in a blue dress. Johnny had told her to keep it informal, and she did. The dress clung to her slender figure, and was set off by the large yellow orchid he'd got for her. She wore no jewellery apart from a single yellow coral slide in her hair.

Sheer silk stockings and neat blue shoes completed her dress. And when Johnny saw her he whistled, said: 'Gee, honey, you'll bust his eyes open! You'll make the dame he's got along look like an old rag. I know it.'

She kissed him clingingly. She knew she looked too flashy; and she also knew that he liked her that way. That's why she didn't care if her dress transgressed the tastes she'd been brought up to respect.

Just as long as Johnny liked it; that was all that mattered now. In the two weeks she'd known him, although he hadn't ever said he loved her, and she hadn't told him her feelings with regard to him, she knew they both felt the same inside.

He wasn't demonstrative. That was a thing that couldn't be helped. She wanted him, and you couldn't have everything, and if he didn't make love to her she took it with a good grace, for on the other hand he hadn't ever suggested anything to her about their sleeping together. He knew she was not yet that far gone, knew she wanted a marriage ceremony before she'd entertain any notion of that, and as yet he wasn't ready for marriage for a while.

They arrived at the Athenia at seven prompt by cab.

As they stepped out and Johnny paid the cabby, a super Cadillac rolled up noiselessly and swooshed to a halt beside the curb.

Corvet and a girl stepped out of it.

Johnny muttered: 'That's the fat swine now. Before long we'll be ridin' around in a heap like that, and Corvet'll be taking his last ride in a hearse!'

She shuddered at the venom in his voice.

Greetings were traded and they went inside the Athenia. Olly Lee bustled forward in a tea gown, a peculiar contrast to the spurious Greek wall paintings.

He bowed to them, took them through into a back room, which was softly lighted, and laid for dinner for four. They smoked and talked awhile before the dinner.

The girl with Corvet was a cheap type, a typical gang-man's floozie. She displayed silk-clad legs and shadow bosom to great advantage. Once or twice Stella noted, with a pang of jealousy, that Johnny looked at her hard whenever she chanced to bend forward.

Stella was something else to Corvet. This was something he'd never known before: a young and seemingly innocent girl tangled in with a racketeer. He wondered just what her position was.

Johnny had introduced her as his 'secretary.'

Corvet doubted that. But he could see she wasn't a regular 'moll.'

His eyes went on a roving commission up from her dainty shoes, along her silken legs, past her hips where the dress pulled tight, across the hollow of her throat and to her young, inexperienced face.

He decided that when he'd had Johnny bumped he'd see what he could — er — do. Perhaps she'd throw in with him then!

They talked about the new pin machines, and Corvet arranged to have his men pick them up and install them the following day. Then Johnny said: 'How about the North section where it joins the Patch? Who controls that territory?'

Corvet said: 'Guy named Bats O'Reilly.'

'Irishman?'

'Irish descent. We don't wanta fool with Bats — he's plenty tough!'

7

A Big Shot

Johnny looked at him coldly: 'I thought *you* were a big shot.'

Corvet wobbled and seemed uncomfortable. Said: 'Yeah, yeah — but you don't understand. The gang boys round this territory got an agreement — we each got our own territory an' we don't bust in on no other guy's joints. It's been that way for ten years, ever since we found we couldn't fight each other an' duck the cops also.'

Johnny grunted: 'Then it's about time some new arrangements was made. I'm goin' up, Corvet! Stick alongside an' you'll go up with me — get gun-jitter an' you'll most likely go down!'

Corvet opened his mouth to say his piece, then shut it. After all why not listen to the guy? Couldn't do any harm — and maybe *he'd* have him bumped before he'd had a chance to do any harm.

'Shoot, Carter,' he said.

'I'm goin' up like I say. I got ambition — and I'm set on windin' up at the top of all the racket in London. That's my aim — an' I generally get my way.'

Corvet grinned: 'Now you're just blowing hot air,' he said: 'An' why? I'll tell ya; because there's over twenty territories in London, and eight of 'em are bigger than mine . . . '

'Ours!' snapped Johnny.

'Okay, ours, then. Eight of 'em have got more boys and smart leaders back of them. We wouldn't stand a chance to crab their business, see.'

'We can try — an' don't forget we got the element of surprise with us. They won't be expectin' any ruckus in face of this here agreement you got with them.'

'I still say you're nuts. But what you plan to do first?'

'We'll make a start on Bats O'Reilly's territory. Suppose you give me the lowdown?'

Corvet thought a moment, then said: 'Bats runs the three clubs on Victoria

Street. They're reckoned to be clubhouses for workin' guys, but they're cram full o' pin tables. You maybe know there's been a heap of trouble lately, what with morality societies tryin' their damnedest to get the pin-halls cleaned up, sayin' they're a menace to our growin' youth an' all that spiel. The cops ain't actually done anythin' yet, but it's gettin' so we got to have a blind here — we can't call a spade a spade no more, and likewise we can't call a pin table arcade a pin table arcade.'

'Yeah, I figure I know that. Things was goin' the same way when I left — '

'When you left *where*?' prompted Corvet.

'Skip it. It's the same all over the country, I reckon. Go on about O'Reilly.'

'He runs these three clubs, and controls the pin machines in about fifteen saloons, an' stores an' tea bars. His ground starts at the west end of Sussex Street an' extends about quarter of a mile in a square.'

'An' you say he's — tough?'

'About as tough as they come. I guess he's the only one who still has the nerve to defy the cops openly and chance gettin' away with it.'

'How's he situated for gunmen?'

'None of us have regular gunmen no more — we have a few uglies just to keep matters under control — but not lead throwers.'

'Mean your own boys can't handle shooters?'

'Oh, yeah, they can handle 'em all right. But they know what's good for 'em an' they don't!'

'An' how about when you want somebody removed?' said Johnny, giving him a penetrating stare.

Corvet fidgeted. Then said: 'It ain't often that happens.'

'But sometimes it does, huh? It does happen sometimes? Say you was anxious to have someone rubbed out — say me, for instance. You've got a regular killer in the mob, ain't you?'

Corvet licked his lips, then nodded: 'I guess any killin's on the side would be handed to Beelzebub, Carter. But ya know we wouldn't dream o' eliminatin' you!'

'You better not,' Johnny warned him. 'I'm a hard guy to eliminate, an' I might decide to do a bit of rubbing out personal if anyone got clever with me. So this Beelzebub is your gun hand, huh?'

Corvet licked his lips. Said: 'Er, yeah.'

'That's okay, then. You leave this Bats guy to me — tell your man to come over to my flat tomorrow mornin', 'bout ten. Tell him he's to take his orders from me for the day.'

'What you gonna do, Carter?'

'Maybe I'll be able to tell you tomorrow night — I got vague ideas that the way to get to the head o' this business is to make a move no one was expectin'. Maybe it won't work on this Bats O'Reilly, but it's worth a try.'

They parted soon after that, and the woman with Corvet handed Johnny a big smile. She said: 'Good night, handsome. An' say — if ever you're round my way drop in, huh? I'd be glad to see a cute bundle o' muscles like yourself, in private . . . '

'I don't mess with anyone else's personal property,' Johnny told her, shortly. 'You better stick to Corvet.'

'I ain't Corvet's lady love,' she grinned. 'I ain't anybody's steady. I just drift around from one guy to another, you know my type. I don't belong . . . but I sure wouldn't mind belonging to any gent like you, big boy. Don't forget, if ever you feel lonely just call on lil' Rita . . . '

And she leaned forward and kissed him, throwing her arms about his neck. Johnny detached her without emotion. Corvet scowled from inside the car, growled: 'Hey, Rita, who you out with? Come on!'

'Go on, sister,' Johnny said. 'You'll have your meal ticket gettin' sore at you.'

She pouted, said: 'Okay — but don't forget if you're ever around — good night handsome — ' She looked at Stella, said: 'An' good night to you — er — Miss 'Secretary'!'

Stella flushed. She was aware of Corvet's lewd eyes grinning in back of the car, and she hated the sneer on Rita's face. It was all too plain what they thought. She half turned away.

The car rolled off, and Johnny said: 'I

feel like air. Let's stroll.'

They strolled, and he talked of his plans. She didn't say anything to him, just kept glancing sideways at him occasionally, very busy with her own thoughts. At last he stopped and stared at her by the light of a street lamp.

'What's eatin' you, babe?'

She didn't answer, hardly heard him.

'Wake up, kid. What's wrong?'

'Oh, I was just — just thinking, Johnny.'

'About what?'

She made a gesture: 'You're getting in deep. Too deep. Why not throw it all up and make a fresh start?'

He stared at her: 'Don't you wanna have swell furs an' jewels an' cars, kid?'

'Not if you have to get them this way. Please, Johnny, for my sake, give it up — let's be two ordinary people — you could get a job . . . '

'Doin' what?' he snorted. 'Mindin' babies?'

'No. A *man's* job — something like — well, railroading, or construction work . . . they're crying out for labour . . . '

He grunted: 'Naw, thanks! I can't picture myself handlin' a pick an' shovel, kiddo. Not yours.'

Desperately she clutched his arm: 'Then I'll get work, Johnny. I'll get my old job back again — I make enough to keep both of us.'

He gripped her arm until it hurt. Said: 'You ever figured I'm that kind of a louse? You think I'd pimp — that's what it comes to.'

'What does it matter? I wouldn't mind supporting you — and it'd be better than what you're doing right now, wouldn't it?'

He released her arm suddenly. His face was moody. He said: 'I'm doing what I'm doing for the both of us. I'm hittin' the top in the rackets here. I figured I'd get a little thanks — but seemingly I ain't. Okay, sister, if you're so darn squeamish, suppose you go back to your old job yourself?'

She looked at him; she whispered: 'Johnny! Is that all you think of me?'

He said: 'Dames aren't important in my life. If I wanted I could have half a dozen, a dozen like Rita any day. An' they got a whole lot more on the ball than you have . . . I asked you before you threw in with me if you had any scruples. You said you'd forget 'em . . . '

She flashed: 'How was I to know you meant to go *this* far?'

'That's jake. No one's stoppin' you leavin' right now. Go on, go ahead an' blow, kid. That's okay. Maybe you'll meet some nice honest guy before long an' settle down with him. That's what you want, ain't it? Marriage an' kids an' one of them little cottages out in the country where your husband'll be able to break his back an' encourage his rheumatics by diggin' the garden an' mowin' the lawn every Sunday. Yeah, that's just what you want — an' I can't give it to you. So go ahead — walk out — '

She bit her lip; she stood staring at him. He turned his back on her and started walking away, quickly.

Tears welled in her eyes and she turned the other way. She could hardly see, everything was swimming before her. He was going, and this was the crucial moment in her life. She could go too, or

110

she could go back — turn, and run back, and never try to argue again.

Or she could walk on, forget him — but could she forget him? He'd become more than just a companion — more than a lover — he was a disease, a disease that had eaten into her heart and made her incapable of feeling happy without him!

A small voice inside her was saying go on and walk right out of his life, he can't bring you anything but trouble . . .

Keep walking, don't look back, forget him, take up where you left off when you met him, you won't always be lonely, you'll meet someone else.

But there was another voice, too, growing stronger. It wasn't the voice of reason this time. It was the voice of emotion.

Turn round, kid, run back, run back like all hell. Tell him you didn't mean what you said, you wouldn't want him any way but the way he is now, that you'll do anything he says and be anything he wants, even if he wants you as a hot water bottle!

Reason said: Don't — he'll bring you

no good. His life wasn't meant for you; you aren't Rita's kind and never will be — don't go back now —

But the other voice came stronger still, until reason became a faint, forgotten echo, and she could hear the command hammering in her mind. Hurry, before it's too late. Go to him and say how sorry you are — tell him how much you love him — that you just don't care so long as you're with him, that's all that counts — that can *ever* count! Do that now . . . hurry.

Johnny had paused by a lamp to light a cigarette. And suddenly she was in his arms, eyes damp with tears, lips parted and face upturned beseechingly, panting, between sobs: 'Oh Johnny, Johnny, I couldn't leave you. I can't. I'm sorry, Johnny . . . I'll be anything you want . . . as long as I'm with you. I don't care!'

He'd been feeling low himself, and not sure why. And now that she'd returned he felt a wave of gladness, and knew that if she hadn't taken the initiative, he would have.

He held her tight in his arms and found

strange words coming from his parted lips, with his quickened breath. Words he hadn't ever used before, and which were coming from a part of him that wasn't ruled by any sense of embarrassment.

'I love you, kid, you know that! I wouldn't leave you — I couldn't do without you any more than you could do without me. That's the way it is, kid, that's it.

'Listen, don't cry, baby. Everything'll be okay. Once I've got some mazuma together I'll throw over the rackets and we'll beat it to the new mown hay and live it out quiet there.

'Don't cry anymore, honey. Forget I ever said what I did. I wouldn't have any truck with a cheap floozie like Rita, you know that. I was just mad — you got more than Rita ever had right in the tip of your little nose, sugar. C'mon now, dry off — '

He held her closer still, felt her trembling in his arms. He pressed his lips to hers hard, and slowly her sobs died away.

She looked up at him and there was a

glad light in her eyes. She said: 'I — I thought you meant it, Johnny. I thought you were tired of me . . . when you said those things.'

'Nuts. I'll tell you what, kid — I'll meet you half way. I *can't* settle down, it isn't the kinda life for me. But I figure this way we're livin' ain't doin' either of us any good. We ought to be together, as if we was married . . . we ought to be living together.'

She spoke, and her voice was very small: 'I hadn't wanted to do anything like that, Johnny . . . I still had that much of my self-respect left.'

'I know you did, baby.'

'I wanted — oh, I wanted everything to be clean and decent with us, even if you were leading the kind of life you do lead.'

'Sure you did, an' that's just why — ' he began.

She stopped him saying anything and held him tighter.

'That's how I wanted things to be with us. You understand, don't you? I'm not — not like Rita. I couldn't be like her. But I'm trying hard, so very hard, to adjust myself to your ways and to be a good 'moll' . . . '

He grinned, began: 'I don't want you like Rita — hell, I don't want you to be like that dame . . . '

She said: 'I can't do without you, Johnny. I — I've been thinking it over — and if it's really what you want — to go all the way and live together I mean — if you want it, I do too.'

He gripped her shoulder, said: 'Kid, you don't mean that?'

She hung her head, nodded. He said: 'Forget it. I wouldn't do that to you. Nope, like I've been saying, I'll meet you half way. I couldn't work *and* settle down — but I can *marry you!*'

8

Action

Johnny braked the rental car fifty miles outside the city limits in a tiny hamlet by the name of Startfold.

Population 2,000; area two square miles, mostly farmland.

He grunted: 'The guy in the U-drive garage said there was a preacher about here some place. According to him it's the biggest house in the main street.'

She protested again, as she had been doing ever since he'd whirled her off her feet into the car.

'Johnny, we haven't a license, we haven't prepared; we haven't a *ring*.'

'Leave me to handle that, kiddo. Here's a dump looks like it may be the right house — yeah look, Rev. Harper, on the brass plate. Okay — in we go.'

They went up to the door and Johnny hammered a few bars on the iron knocker. He growled: 'These hicks! Fifty miles only out of London, and they haven't even a doorbell.'

A window shot up over their heads. A man called: 'Er — what is it? Who's down there?'

Johnny said: 'You the Rev?'

'I am the Reverend, yes. Why?'

'There's a guy down here needs a guy like you. Dyin', he is. Been in a road smash — hurry it up, will ya, Rev?'

'Bless my soul! I'll be right down.'

His head popped back in; they heard him bustling about. Then steps on the stairs, along the passage. The door opened. Johnny pushed in.

The Reverend, a bald-headed, round-faced old man, panted: 'Where is the poor dear man? Where is he? Quickly, so that I may offer him consolation . . . '

Johnny grinned: 'I'm right here, Rev!'

'What? But — young man, you said a man was dying!'

'He is — I am. Dyin' to get hitched, so speed it up will ya and make us two one!'

The minister gaped at him, and slowly

an angry glare came over his cherubic countenance.

'How dare you sir!' he grated. 'What *damn* — er — what *earthly* right have you to burst in here in this manner by use of a vile and deplorable ruse, and then inform me that you merely wish to get married? I repeat . . . '

'Cool off, Rev. Your shirt's burnin' an' my temper's gettin' short — it ain't good at the best of times. Do just like I tell you an' it's worth twenty quid to you.'

The Reverend thawed visibly. '*Har! Harrumph*! Er — if you are in so much of a hurry, young man . . . I . . . er — yes, I think I can accommodate you.'

'We don't want accommodatin'. Just marryin'. Okay?'

'I — yes. Very well — er — I will call my wife and my maid to serve as witnesses. One minute.'

He called up the stairs: 'Evangeline, kindly call Gertrude and bring her down here to act as witness to a wedding. Come yourself, dear, too.'

He came back to Johnny, beamed at him. He said: 'I have a small private altar arranged in the front parlor. If you'd care to step in there . . . '

They stepped in there. He said: 'And now, young man, if I may have your license . . . ?'

Johnny said: 'We ain't got a license, Rev. Didn't have time.'

'What? Then I'm afraid I can't help you . . . '

'I figured you could get hitched over the limits minus a say-so in writing?'

'That ruling does not apply here, young man. I'm sorry . . . '

Johnny said: 'You'll be sorry if you *don't* marry us, Pop!'

The Reverend Harper gulped and eyed the gun as though mesmerized.

Johnny said: 'Yep, it's a shooter, Rev. Now, how about it?'

'I-yi-yi-yi-yi — '

'Quit doin' bird imitations and start singing your sermon.'

The Rev raised horrified hands, and shook his head. He gazed at the gun with popping eyes, stuttered: 'You're jug-jug-joking.'

'Nope, there ain't any rib about it, Pop. I guess you've officiated at plenty o' *shotgun weddings* in your younger days, huh? Well, this is a shotgun weddin' with a difference. Get it?'

'But I can't . . . think . . . think of my position. My high position . . . in the church!'

'You'll have a low position in the churchyard if you don't haul your braces up an' start singing!'

He jabbed the Minister tolerantly in the stomach.

The Reverend's wife, an angular, horse-faced woman of about forty-eight, came into the room, the maid trudging behind her. The maid spotted the gun and gave a shrill scream, then flopped backwards onto the floor in a swoon. The Reverend's wife thundered: '*What* is *this?*'

The Reverend gulped: 'These two young people — er — wish to be married . . . '

'Then why not marry them, Ephraim? That's your *job*, isn't it?'

Ephraim coughed: 'They've offered me twenty pounds, dear, as far as my trouble's concerned. But . . . '

She said: 'Then marry them at once! *At once!* Gertrude, you utterly senseless girl, wake up. The gentleman is only joking.'

The Reverend said: 'No, dear, he isn't joking with *that* gun.'

'What . . . you . . . you mean it's a *real* gun?'

'Unfortunately, dear, it is.'

'But — why?'

'He's trying to force me to marry them, my dear.'

'I shouldn't have thought you'd need any forcing with twenty pounds staring you in the face, Ephraim. We aren't so wealthy we can afford to reject an offer of *that* nature.'

'That isn't the point. They haven't a license and the laws of this country say they should have one. I am imperiling my position if I marry them . . . '

'Good Heavens! No license?'

Johnny said: 'I've stood round about enough cackle, Rev. Now bring that maid round and get us married — or else.'

The Reverend murmured: 'Perhaps you'd better do as he says, dear.'

Mrs. Harper nodded and bent to revive the swooning maid. She was a sensible woman. Twenty pounds for a marriage ceremony was twenty pounds for hardly anything in her opinion, and even if a gun went with it, so what? She started reviving the maid.

Stella tugged Johnny's sleeve, muttered: 'Let's go, Johnny. You can't force these people to marry us . . . it isn't fair.'

'It's quite all right, young woman,' sniffed Mrs. Harper. 'My husband *will* marry you. He won't get into trouble — he can say he was forced and that will clear him — Ephraim!'

'Yes, my love?'

'Get your prayer book at once.'

'Yes, my dear.'

He was under her thumb, that was clear. He shuffled to a drawer of a desk at the end of the room. His wife said primly:

'Young man, I'll take that twenty — right now.'

'Sure. Here, lady.'

Johnny handed it to her, and she inserted it in the top of her dress, patted it into position, and sniffed again. She said: 'You can put away your gun young man. Gertrude will be sensible again in a moment, and there is no need to frighten the wits out of the girl.'

122

Looking at Gertrude, Stella wondered if she would ever be sensible, and if she had any remaining wits to be frightened out of.

The Reverend came back then, and Gertrude yelped: 'Oooh! A gun — that man had a gun! I saw it — we'll all be murdered.'

'Nonsense, Gertrude. The man means no harm — do as you're told, girl. You are to witness a ceremony.'

Subdued but fearful, Gertrude stood leaning on the table, quivering. The Reverend opened his book and started the ceremony.

'Have you the ring?'

Johnny slid a signet ring from his finger. 'Make do with this, Rev, will ya?'

The ceremony proceeded, by far the most unusual wedding at which the Rev had ever officiated.

'By the powers invested in me I now declare you man and wife.'

And, he added, as an afterthought: 'May — er — you be very happy.'

Johnny looked at Stella and she looked back at him.

The Reverend smiled for the first time, murmured: 'You may kiss the bride now, young man.'

'Cool,' giggled Gertrude.

'Be silent, girl,' snapped Mrs. Harper.

Johnny said: 'No time for that right now, Rev. We'll make up later. Now we have to be going — '

'Yes, yes, of course . . .'

'After,' said Johnny pointedly, 'you've signed the certificate of marriage!'

'Oh, dear. I hate to — er — put this transaction down on paper. If it ever came to light it would ruin me.'

'It won't come to light. An' I figure unless we have that written statement from you this marriage ain't very legal. So let's have it, Rev.'

He was cornered. He made out the certificate hastily, and the two witnesses signed it. Johnny gave it to Stella. Then he gave the maid a pound and Mrs. Harper a further five.

The Reverend came to the door with them, probably to see they didn't sneak anything on the way out. Johnny turned at the door, shoved a flyer into his hands.

'Thanks, Rev. Seems like your wife collars all the change in this joint — there's something for your trouble.'

The Rev opened his mouth to speak, but they were in the U-drive car and away before he could get it out.

Stella leaned back against the cushions, starry-eyed.

Johnny grinned: 'Sorry it wasn't the kind of a wedding you'd have liked. But when I want to do a thing I want to do it *bad*. I couldn't have waited another three weeks or so . . . '

She said: 'I wouldn't have wanted it any other way — ' but her voice was a little wistful. Then she laughed: 'What does it matter? I've got you, haven't I, and that's what counts most of all.'

He said: 'Happy honey?'

'More than I've ever been, Johnny.'

He cut the engine, bent over and kissed her. She drew a deep breath, said: 'Hey! You're improving, mister!'

He smiled: 'I should. I gotta lot of scope now, ain't I?'

She murmured: 'Johnny, will it always be like this?'

'You mean dashin' around like a coupla scalded cats?'

'No. I mean between us — will you always feel the same about — me?'

'More than you know, sweetheart. So don't worry your pretty head about it. Sorry I can't offer you a honeymoon.'

'Don't be silly. We'll honeymoon at home. You don't have to go away someplace to honeymoon, stupid.'

He said: 'Say, that's right, you don't do you! Let's step on it!'

They dumped the U-drive car outside town. They didn't want to run it right in because the Reverend might have already phoned London and informed the cops about the happenings. That meant the cops would be watching out for U-drive cars at all depots.

They walked in on foot, and the three miles seemed a stride to them, strolling along arm in arm.

They arrived back at their flat. Johnny fitted his key, opened the door. Stella stood outside waiting. Johnny said: 'Okay, babe, come in an' rest your puppies.'

'Oh, Johnny, you are a hopeless husband.'

'I am? Heck, what did I do now?'

''S what you *didn't* do! You're supposed to *carry* me over the threshold, silly. It's a custom.'

Johnny grinned: 'Well, whaddaya know, huh? You'll have to forgive me, kid, for not knowin' these finer points. I guess you'll have to put it down to me not bein' hitched before.'

He picked her up, carried her in lightly.

She said: 'Want anything from the icebox, Johnny?'

'No, kid, I ain't hungry.'

'Tired?'

'Holy Moses no! You ain't are ya?'

'No, I'm not, Johnny. I'll have a drink.'

'Sure.' He poured drinks, and gave one to her. Said: 'Say, I sure got action today, didn't I?'

She smiled: 'I thought the Reverend was going to become airborne when you shoved your gun at him.'

'The old dame didn't waste any valuable time havin' hysterics though. She sure latched onto the twenty quick enough.'

'I felt sorry for the Reverend. He looked so henpecked . . . '

Johnny sobered momentarily: 'Yeah — I guess that's what comes of gettin' married . . .'

She said: 'Johnny, what are you saying?'

'Eh? Shucks, I didn't mean anythin' by that, baby.'

She took his arm, drew him close to her, kissed his ear.

'I know you didn't darling. I'll go in, now . . .'

She got up and went into the bedroom. Johnny looked nervous and fumbled with his tie. A few minutes passed, then: 'Johnny!'

He drained his whisky, and with a do or die expression, staggered to the bedroom.

* * *

Beelzebub blew in the next morning and found Johnny shaving and singing happily. From the kitchen of the flat came an appetizing odour of ham and eggs frying, and Stella's voice: 'Be ready in just a minute, darling.'

Beelzebub grinned, a toothless grin, and yelled: 'Anybody home?'

Johnny heard him and came out.

Beelzebub said: 'Mornin'. You want to lock your doors nights, pal! Corvet give me orders to tag along with you today. Okay?'

'That's the idea,' Johnny told him. 'Bit early, ain't you?'

'It's *you* who's a bit late.'

Johnny looked at the time, said: 'Sure, that's so. I had a big night. Bring your persuader along?'

'Right here,' said Beelzebub, dragging it into view.

At that moment Stella came in with a tray of food. She saw the gun and her face altered. She said: 'Oh, Johnny, what . . . ?'

He took her in his arms and kissed her. He said: 'Relax, kid. He's on our side.'

'Johnny, you aren't going into any — any trouble today?'

'Not unless I can't sidestep it, kid. Got a most particular yen to dodge trouble now. Got something worth dodging it for, huh?'

Beelzebub chuckled: 'Say, you sure can pick your dames, bud.'

Johnny grunted: 'Listen fresh guy, this lady is Mrs. Carter. An' don't forget it.'

'Who am I to argue,' said Beelzebub. 'I'm only the knock off guy in these parts. But I still say you sure can pick 'em.'

He chuckled lasciviously and let his eyes wander up and down Stella in her flimsy, all but transparent negligée. Johnny took his arm and guided him gently but firmly into the other room. He said: 'Sit right here, Beelzebub. You'll be gettin' wrong thoughts in your innocent little noggin. Just behave 'til I finish eatin'.'

Beelzebub occupied the golden minutes by testing his gun. He was always ready for emergencies, was Beelzebub. Short he might be as far as grey matter went, but when it came to drawing and firing before the other guy — well, Beelzebub had had to draw for his life against more guys than he could remember — and he was still living!

Within fifteen minutes Johnny came to the door in a slick pin-stripe suit and a white carnation. Stella hung round his neck, gave him a final kiss, said: 'Please, Johnny, take care of yourself.'

'I'm a cinch. Be back soon as I can, babe.'

They went down the stairs leaving her staring after them with a worried frown. Beelzebub said, as they hit the sidewalk: 'Where we heading?'

'You know your way to O'Reilly's hangout?'

'Bats O'Reilly? You aren't goin' there, are you?'

'Why not?'

'You tell me.'

'Okay, I will. We're going to proposition Bats. We're goin' to tell him about us takin' over his territory . . . '

'We're what?' stuttered Beelzebub.

'Takin' his territory over. And we're goin' to offer him the chance to come in with us, or be blasted out of business. That's why we're goin' to see Bats O'Reilly.'

'Do you know what Bats does to guys who try to heave him?' said Beelzebub, blankly.

'No, what?'

'The river, mate, the river. Or maybe they're found in some quiet country road with their toes turned to Heaven! You walk in an' tell him what you told me an' he'll murder us, just plain murder us!'

'Not,' grunted Johnny, 'if we murder him first! I think I mentioned to you about me havin' a gosh-awful temper, didn't I? Well, for Bat's sake it's to be hoped he doesn't get my goat.'

'You can't do it,' Beelzebub expostulated. 'If we do like you say we're a pair of certs for the morgue, I'm tellin' ya.'

'Are you yeller?'

'Nobody can say that to me,' snarled Beelzebub, gripping his gun harder in his pocket. 'If you . . . '

'Listen, I know you ain't yeller, Beelzy. An' if you stick close to me it'll pay off big . . . '

'Yeah? You're nuts. If I stick close to you it's a sure suicide!'

'That's what you'd've said about me walking in on Corvet with all you boys there yesterday, ain't it? But I'm still alive an' what's more, I'm kickin'.'

'For how long?' grunted Beelzebub. 'Or maybe you think Corvet'll let you get away with it, huh?'

'I know Corvet's plannin' to have me bumped. I heard him say so. I know you've been selected to do the job. But I'm not worried.'

'You ain't? Why not?'

'I'll tell you why; because as of today you don't work for that fat slug no more, Beelzy.'

'I don't? Are you kiddin'? Who do I work for then?'

'You work for me . . . you ain't gettin' a square deal with Corvet, I'll tell ya. What does he pay you?'

'Ten percent of profits.'

'Ten per for the bump off a man, the most important member of the outfit? Why, it's murder, boy, murder!'

'He don't think I'm important. There ain't many killin's to do nowadays,' explained Beelzebub mournfully.

Johnny clapped his back: 'Is that so? Underworked, huh? Well, you throw in with me, Beelzy. You rate twenty per, and there'll be plenty killings to do when I head the outfit. What's more you'll be second top man! Right back of me in everythin'. You'll help run the outfit. What say, Beelzy? Are you in?'

9

Bats Plays Rough

'How about it?' repeated Johnny.

Beelzebub was staring into air. He muttered: 'That fat heel's been kicking me around for the last ten years. He knows gun guys ain't in demand these days, an' he knows there ain't any other outfit I could tag up with in town . . . but he calls me quick enough when he wants somebody puttin' on the spot.'

'Like me, f'rinstance?'

Beelzebub said: 'Yeah — I mean no. Hell, what give you that notion?'

'I know all about it. You were goin' to get the job of bumpin' me, ain't that so?'

Beelzebub said: 'I guess you're right. But — you say if I weld in with you I'll be your right hand?'

'You got the measure. An' you get more dough.'

He said: 'Ya mean I have a say in what the gang does?'

'You'll be somebody, instead of the broken-down second-rate professional killer you are now.'

'Geez! I've always wanted to be somebody. You ain't foolin'?'

'I wouldn't kid you.'

Beelzebub stuck out his hand and Johnny took it. 'I'm right behind ya, boss, from here on. Corvet can go to hell.'

'That's just about where I plan to send him.'

They stopped outside an office building and Beelzebub said: 'Here's our port o' call. This is where the O'Reilly character hangs out. Got an office on the fifth.'

'We'll go right on up.'

They went in; the building was on the shabby side. There was no lift. They started pounding up the stairs. They were panting by the time they reached the fifth. At the far end of the corridor was a frosted glass door which said:

'Fingal O'Reilly; City Enterprises.'

They walked right into the outer office without knocking. There was a mob man at a desk behind a barrier which squared off the inner sanctum. Johnny walked up to him, grunted: 'Announce us will ya, pal?'

The mob man went right on manicuring his nails with the business end of a short knife. He didn't even look up.

He said: 'Bats can't see nobody right now.'

'I said to announce us, mister. We got urgent business.'

He looked up. 'Yeah? What kind? I don't know you.'

'You'll get to in time. Now get moving.'

'Who the hell are you?'

'Names don't matter. Here's my visitin' card.'

He slicked his rod from his pocket and trained it on the mug. The mug said: 'I get it, a tough guy, huh? Okay, mister, maybe you better see Bats after all. He knows how to deal with your kind.'

He unclipped a cheap intercom and said: 'Hey, boss, there's a citizen out here wants to see you. Says it's important, an' he makes his point with a Lucy. How about it?'

O'Reilly's thick Irish accent came back metallically.

'Name o' what?'

'Won't give one. Got Beelzebub from Corvet's outfit along with him.'

'Has he bejasus? Send the man in then.'

The mug said: 'Bats says for you to go in, mister.'

Johnny said: 'Okay.' He leaned over suddenly and switched off the intercom with the muzzle of his gun. He said: 'Lock the door, Beelzy. We don't want no interruptions. An' you, pal, you start hoofin' it in front o' me. I don't like guys back of me when I'm talkin' business.'

The mug gaped. 'Take it easy, mister. I can't jerk into Bats' private office without permission.'

'I'm givin' you permission now. Walk.'

The mug walked. Followed by Johnny's rod and Johnny and Beelzebub, he opened the inner door and went in. Bats was sitting back of the desk there with his gun out. Johnny said: 'You best put that gun to roost, Bats, or maybe I'll let you have it an' keep your receptionist in front o' me as my shield.'

Bats growled: 'Whaddya want, ye spalpeen?'

Johnny retorted: 'A peaceable talk with you. Slide home your gun and nothing happens.'

Bats slung his gun into the opened drawer beside him, said: 'Say what ye got to say, an' make it short, divil ye!'

He was lean and long and far from the type of man Johnny had expected. But there was Irish written all over him and the set of his jaw told he had a stubborn streak.

Johnny said: 'Keep this runt covered, Beelzy, while I chat with Bats.'

Beelzebub obliged and Johnny went over until he was in front of the desk. He leaned slightly forward, said: 'You know Corvet had amalgamated with me?'

'I don't get it.'

'We're workin' together for now . . . I'm helpin' run his territory. We're brushin' up the whole pin table racket.'

Bats said: 'Yeah? What's that to me?'

'Plenty. We're expandin', also. We're takin' over *your* ground.'

138

Bats sat upright, snapped: 'The divil take ye fust, man! I'll see ye in hell afore ye'd get my territory.'

Johnny said: 'Maybe you will see somebody in hell, Bats, but it won't be me! Unless you play ball you'll be there a whole long time before I arrive.'

Bats said: 'We got an agreement . . . '

'Forget it. Those agreements don't stand any more. Come in with us — between the three of us we can wipe out the rest of the mobs and make a three way split.'

Bats stared at him: said: 'A monopoly eh? Organized crime.'

'Sure. Why not?'

'I don't want any part of it at all. Take your propositions somewhere else with ye man.'

Johnny said: 'If you don't come in it's going to be very tough for you!'

Bats' hand moved closer to the drawer containing the gun. Johnny slammed the barrel of his gun forward, jammed it on the gang man's fingers. Bats cursed loudly.

'Don't get rough,' Johnny warned him.

'I told you we came very peaceably. I'm askin' you again if you'll come in?'

'No!'

'Okay. That's okay if you want it the hard way. Look out, Bats. It's coming your way pretty soon . . . when you get a few of them clubs of yours blasted by pineapples you'll maybe think again an' decide different. If you don't, we'll have to see about havin' *you* blasted by a pineapple!'

O'Reilly said: 'Not if I blast you fust, ye rogue, ye!'

He seemed resigned; but suddenly he heaved the desk upwards taking Johnny in the guts. Johnny staggered slightly and O'Reilly followed up his advantage by leaning over and slamming a hard left to Johnny's jaw. Johnny simply shook his head, without losing his wits. He saw Bats' hand streaking for his gun . . . and he picked up a heavy inkstand and slashed it swiftly at Bats' face.

Bats staggered backwards with a yell, sat down. Ink and blood flowed down from his cut forehead. Johnny went round and slammed shut the desk drawer. He said: 'They told me you was tough — but you're just a dope in my estimation. Try anything like that again and you'll be a *dead* dope!'

Bats glared furiously at him, said: 'This is one time you've gone too fur, mister. I don't know who you are or where Corvet dug ye up from. But you don't do *that* to Bats O'Reilly an' get away wid it.'

Johnny mimicked his thick accent: 'Bejavers, have ye no sense at arl, at arl? Can ye not see man, that 'twill be mortal hard on ye if ye don't do like I'm telling ye? Come in — once we've lined up your territory we can go ahead and drag the Loop District into line.'

'I told ye I don't want nothin' to do wi' it at all. Now get out of here.'

Johnny said: 'Okay. You asked for it.'

Swiftly he reversed his gun, slammed it down on top of the Irishman's head. Bats groaned and slumped. Johnny said: 'Stroke that mug down, Beelzy.'

'Sure boss.'

The other thug went down in answer to Beelzebub's down stroke. Johnny looked at Bats. He grinned: 'Maybe that'll help him realize I ain't playin'. Come on, let's go.'

* * *

'How'd ya make out?' queried Corvet, peering craftily at Johnny who had dropped into his private rooms. Johnny said: 'Not so good. We're goin' to have to fight it out with Bats.'

'Why not leave him alone?' suggested Corvet. 'We don't want to kick up any trouble with O'Reilly.'

'I'll kick up plenty if he don't see reason. Forget Bats for now. I come to see you about somethin' else . . . '

Corvet's eyes narrowed: 'Yeah? What else is botherin' you?'

Johnny grunted: 'What kinda flowers was you plannin' to send when they lay me under?'

'Are you nuts?' Corvet stared. 'What makes you think they're goin' to lay you under?'

'I don't think — I know they ain't. But you figure it won't be so long before

142

Peter's turnin' me away from the Pearly Gates, don't you?'

Corvet spread his hands helplessly. 'Search me. I don't even know what you're talkin' about, so help me!'

Johnny drew his lips back from his teeth. He grated: 'Listen, Corvet. I'm good an' mad with you! I didn't want to mention this on account of I wanted you to think ya had me fooled — but I can't bottle up no longer. It's comin' out — I heard what ya said 'bout havin' me bumped by Beelzy. How about that?'

Corvet went white. He said: 'You been hearin' things!'

'Sure, I been hearin' things. An' I also heard them from Beelzy hisself!'

'Why that no-good dirty — '

'You can lay off Beelzy, see. He works for me now, not you. I'm givin' you one more warnin', Corvet. Keep your nose clean — you're here to do what you're told now. I'm the big shot — don't forget that! I had an idea your boys weren't too satisfied with the way you ran things, an' I've talked to 'em. They were easy. They all work for me as of today.'

'You're lyin',' panted Corvet coming to his feet. 'They ain't the kind who'd sell me out!'

Johnny grunted: 'Ask them. I figure they'd have shoved you out sooner or later, anyway. The days when you could scare the hell out of them is gone. You're fat an' flabby and you've lost your trigger speed. Furthermore, you've developed into a yellow belly through havin' things too easy. You'd be surprised just how quick your hoods were to jump at the chance of workin' for me — more so when they heard about the bigger cuts of the profits they'd get!'

'Get bigger — bigger cuts? But — '

'They get *your* cut divided among them!'

'My cut?'

'That's what I said. You might as well know right now that I meant to have you bumped sooner or later. Now I'm givin' you a chance to blow — to get out whilst you can! I didn't figure things'd be as easy as they have. But your boys played in nice. They're with me. So you don't have to be bumped after all. I'm givin' you

144

until tonight to beat it . . . if you're here when I get back, it'll be too bad for you, Corvet!'

Corvet sat still and silent. He was thinking — thinking that if it had been so easy for Johnny to buy his boys, they'd sell him out again just as easy. He might still be able to turn the tables and buy them back!

Johnny went on: 'I got no more to say. You can start packin' an' beat it, an' feel thankful you still got your health an' strength, such as it is!'

He gave Corvet one last menacing stare and walked out.

⋆ ⋆ ⋆

Corvet sat for a long time, his fists resting on his fat knees to prevent them trembling. No one came near him; his boys were keeping clear. Maybe they were a bit ashamed of the way they'd rounded on him. Maybe — but Corvet doubted it.

At last the telephone rang, bringing him from his mental stupor.

He grasped the receiver.

'Corvet here . . . '

'Corvet? This is O'Reilly. Bats O'Reilly.'

'O'Reilly! Yeah — '

'Who the divil's this guy that called on me today? An' what th' hell are you playing at? If you're tryin' to break the agreements we made you'll get more trouble than you can handle!'

Corvet said: 'Listen, Bats, I ain't anything to do with anything anymore. I've just been thrown out, washed up. My own men threw in with this bastard, and I get the gate.'

Bats said: 'Say, is that on the level?'

'I wouldn't fool about it. He just walked in an' bust up the whole game in the last few days. He just told me to go to hell and clear out . . . '

Bats whistled: 'Phew! The divil you say?'

'I'm pledgin' it,' said Corvet.

Bats said: 'Then why don't you gun him down?'

Corvet mumbled: 'He'd be a nasty guy to shoot it out with.'

Bats deliberated a minute. Said: 'You levellin' with me?'

'Why would I be sayin' all this if not?

Sure, I'm straight. It's just like I said. What's more he intends to blast you an' the rest of the gangs outa business . . . '

Bats grunted: 'That's what he told me when he called. Well, I ain't lost my nerve yet, if certain other spalpeens have. What's his address? Where does he stay at? An' how many strong arms does he keep on the joint?'

Corvet tensed, said, eagerly: 'He don't keep any hoods on the premises. There's only me an' Beelzy know his address. He lives in an apartment in the Grantland block.'

'That's swell.'

Corvet said: 'Are you — goin' to do anythin' about him?'

'Maybe . . . '

Bats hung up; and Corvet, feeling that Johnny's day was drawing to a close, went out to locate his boys and try to buy them back again!

★   ★   ★

'I told you not to worry, baby,' Johnny grinned, kissing Stella as she clung to the lean, strong length of him, on his return.

'Just relax an' leave it to me. Everythin's swell, kid. Believe me. I've bought Corvet's boys out an' I'm toppin' the mob now.'

She said: 'And how about Corvet, Johnny? He's mean — he'll try to hurt you — '

'Corvet lost his nerve a long time ago. He's scared of cops, scared of rival gang bosses, an' he's scared of me. He'll blow. He won't have nerve enough to try anythin'!'

She shook her head and pressed her lips softly against his cheek: 'I hope not; I couldn't live any more if something happened to you, Johnny. I don't want to harp on it, but . . . '

He slapped her on the rump playfully, said: 'Then don't, kid. I know you're goin' to ask me to toss it all overboard again, but I can't. I was cut out for this. I'm goin' places an' doin' big things. Before I'm through they'll call me King of the Cockneys — an' I'll need my Queen . . . '

He stopped and looked surprised, said:

'Hey, did that come from me?'

'It did, Johnny. You're getting quite poetic.'

He kissed her again. 'Maybe that's because I'm so happy, kid. I'm happier than I ever remember bein' before. That's on account of you, sugar.'

She released him, said: 'Dinner's ready.'

They ate, and lingered over coffee. Then he got up, said: 'Okay, kitten. Go get your glad rags on and we'll make way for the bright lights an' hot music.'

She nodded and made for the bedroom. There was a ring at the door. Johnny said: 'I'll get it.' She heard him opening it, then heard Beelzebub's strained voice:

'Boss, Corvet's buyin' back the boys! I just overheard him — ya better get down there quick!'

10

Into the Night

Stella glanced at the clock for the umpteenth time, and took to pacing up and down again. Johnny had rushed right out with Beelzebub, hadn't even stopped to say so long. He'd been gone almost two hours now, and she was sick with worry.

On a sudden impulse she turned to a drawer and took from it one of his spare guns. She examined it to see if it was loaded. It was. She slipped it down the top of her dress, shivering as the cold metal touched her soft warm skin.

Then she went into the bedroom and slipped out from the house coat, and selected the most serviceable skirt she had.

★   ★   ★

Bats O'Reilly said: 'It's okay, I can handle the divil. I'll go alone — too many cooks spoil the broth — '

His second in command shrugged, said: 'You want to be careful, Bats. Shoot first . . . '

'Sure, take it easy, Donovan. There'll be but the one shot.'

He walked out, attired in dark coat, hat and rubber-soled sneakers. He walked swiftly along the road taking the shortest route to the Grantland apartment building.

The lower passage was well lighted, but empty. He took stock then eased quickly into the electric elevator. He got in and thumbed the button that said: 'ROOF.'

The elevator shot up and decanted him on the broad flat roof of the apartment. No one else was up there.

A fire escape ladder ran down from the parapet past the windows. He lowered himself gently over the side on to the rungs and started climbing downwards.

He gained the first dark window and peered in. He could see nothing of the room. Six feet along from him was another window with a light on. There was a ledge running along the sheer wall and he found that by gripping the ornamental stonework over his head and sliding his feet sideways along the six inch ledge, he could move along to the lighted window. He did so.

A young woman was there, a woman whose beauty made Bats' hardened arteries pump blood more freely. She was pacing up and down, restlessly. Of Johnny there was no sign.

He was about to try the other window cautiously, when a light inside snapped on. He froze . . .

The girl was inside there now, taking off the house coat. She took a skirt from the bedrail, then opened the doors of a large wall wardrobe apparently to select a sweater or blouse. She had to go right inside to get it.

And with one jerk he had the window up and was in the room with his gun in hand!

Stella jumped with alarm. She dropped the things she was holding and stood staring blankly at the man who had entered by the window. Who he was or what he wanted she had no idea. But he was holding a gun, and he looked mean —

She became aware that she was scantily dressed. She made a move towards the bed —

She gasped: 'Who are you? What do you want?'

'Me name's O'Reilly, Bats O'Reilly.'

She gave a start of surprise and trepidation. He murmured: 'I see you know of me.'

She didn't answer, stood staring at him wide eyed. He said: 'You can guess why I'm here? I want that thafe an' rogue called Carter. Where is he?'

She stammered: 'Jo — Johnny isn't here. He — he isn't coming back here again.'

He glanced round, smiled: 'Then why did he leave all his clothes scattered around, me dear?'

She bit her lip. Said: 'I'm sendin' them on for him.'

'Indade? An' isn't that thoughtful av ye, now? But ye won't fool me, young woman. 'Tis lyin' yez are, I can tell.'

'I'm not!' she cried. 'Honestly, Johnny won't be back.'

'Johnny won't, won't he, the darlin' boy! 'T'would be a pity to miss him — so I'm thinkin' I'll wait afther arl!'

His Irish accent was coming strong. It always did when he was keyed up. He said: 'Arl I have to do is to find somethin' to fix you with — '

'What are you going to do to — to Johnny?' she shivered.

'What Johnny was plannin' to do to me. I'll be shootin' the dear boy. But I'll make it quick, me darlin'. He won't suffer.'

He looked round the room and his eyes fell on the wardrobe. He said: 'Have ye the key to this?'

She looked towards the sideboard. He went over there and picked up a bunch of keys. Her eyes followed him and whilst he was momentarily distracted she raised her hand to her chest and slid the gun from its resting place.

All she was conscious of was that Johnny would come walking back right into Bats' muzzle! She had to stop it. Even if it meant — *murder*.

154

Bats hadn't been watching her too closely. He hadn't suspected that she already had a weapon concealed on her, not dressed as she was now. That was why he looked so surprised when, as he was turning, the slugs ripped into him!

There was a sudden knocking at the door. A male voice said: 'Is everything all right in there?'

It was the porter. The night porter. In a panic she rushed to the door and shot the bolt. He must have heard it. He called: 'I heard firing. Is that Mister Carter? What's happened here?'

She stood perfectly still hardly daring to draw a breath. He went on: 'Open this door, sir. Do you hear? I heard gunfire from here.'

Still she remained silent.

He snapped: 'Unless you open this door I shall be forced to call the police!'

She heard him muttering angrily, then heard his steps dying away hurriedly down the corridor. He was going down to telephone to the police! Now what had she done?

Steps came back towards the door.

Stopped. The handle was tried. Someone knocked. She waited, hand to mouth.

Johnny called: 'Kid — what's wrong? Are you there? Let me in, kid!'

With a cry of relief she opened the door and fell into his arms. He stared at her, said: 'What . . . ?'

'Oh, Johnny, Johnny. I thought you'd been killed! That awful Bats O'Reilly came here . . . he meant to wait for you and kill you . . . '

'What?'

'I — I shot him, Johnny! I feel horrible! The — the porter — he heard the shots — he's gone to call the police!'

Johnny grunted: 'Hell, that caps it! Where is Bats?'

'In — in the bedroom . . . '

Johnny rushed over, went inside. When he came back he was carrying a skirt, sweater, and coat. He threw them to her, said: 'Into those kid, quick. We're leavin'!'

She whispered: 'Is — is he dead?'

He nodded silently. He said: 'You did that for me, Stella?'

'He was going to — kill you,' she shivered.

Johnny said: 'Thanks, kid. I won't forget it. Don't feel too badly. He was just another rat.'

She was struggling into the coat. She said: 'I was frantic with worry, Johnny. Where've you been? What happened?'

'When I got back there Corvet had half the boys sold on going back in with him. It came to a showdown, and I drew my gun — they all drew and we shot it out in the room. I got Corvet, but Beelzy got plugged. We were still blazing away at each other when I heard police sirens. I made a bolt for it the back way, came back here. But the cops'll get to know who I am an' where I'm at now, from the survivors. That's why we got to leave here, anyway — and what with Bats . . . '

There was another knock at the door. Johnny called: 'Yeah?'

'Oh, you're in, Mister Carter! This is the porter — I heard shots from your room — couldn't get any answer. I was afraid that something had happened . . . '

Johnny opened the door. The porter peered in. Johnny said: 'We just got back. Did you say there were shots from here?'

'Yes, I've just called the police. Must have gone down in one elevator whilst you were going up in the other. They'll be here in a few minutes to look around.'

Johnny nodded 'Maybe we've had burglars. Suppose you take a swivel round yourself?'

The porter stepped in, nodding. He got one stride past Johnny when Johnny hit him suddenly with clenched fists on the nape of the neck. The porter went down as if he'd been slugged with a sandbag.

Johnny grabbed hold of Stella's hand, said: 'C'mon, kid, we have to move now, the flatties'll be here anytime.' Johnny grunted: 'Fire escape, quick!'

They hit the iron escape and, Stella first, they almost tumbled down. The side of the apartment block was deserted, and they went round to the front at a run. Outside the building two police patrol cars were parked.

And *both* were still running!

Johnny rushed for the front one the moment he saw they were both unattended. He piled in, motioning Stella into the seat beside him.

He knew one or two spots round London. He headed for a large forest some eighty miles distant, driving the car to its limit.

He said to Stella: 'Up here there is a cabin, used in the huntin' season. Now it'll be deserted. We can lie low there until they decide to take the road blocks they'll put up against us, down.'

The cabin was a one-storey affair with a single room. The windows were cracked and stuffed with paper. But they dumped the car in a clump of thickets behind, and went inside. Johnny said: 'Settle down, kid.'

Stella murmured: 'Johnny, they'll get us . . . '

He was loading his guns and examining the shotguns he'd taken from the rear of the patrol car. He said: 'Not alive!'

★   ★   ★

The motorcycle cop watched the large car cut off from the road into the forest. The driver hadn't noticed him.

He wondered curiously why anyone

should want to take a forest trail which led nowhere but to a clearing, and decided it wasn't his business anyway. It was a right of way, and maybe they were just a necking couple seeking shelter.

But about two hours later when he reported to the station house and heard they were blocking all roads and he was wanted for extra duty to try and get a couple who'd bust off in a police car, he remembered that the car he'd seen, dimly, in the gloom, had looked very suspiciously like a squad car!

And one hour after that the police closed in on the cabin in the woods, and found the dumped car behind the cabin about a hundred feet away!

★　★　★

Johnny said: 'Kid — kid, wake up. There's somebody moving out here!'

As she reached his side he whipped out his gun, shouted: 'Who's that out there?'

There was a momentary silence; then: 'Okay, Carter! We know all about you — an' we found a body in your flat. That was the woman's work according to the statements we took . . . '

Johnny shouted: 'Nuts! The dame didn't kill anyone; I killed Bats O'Reilly.'

'That won't wash. We found out you couldn't have got back from the shooting at Corvet's place in time to have killed Bats before we arrived. Anyway the prints on the gun we found'll prove who did it. You got enough to answer for without adding more. We got an idea you're wanted in Liverpool for murder.'

Johnny snarled: 'Hold it! Come any closer an' I start firin'!'

'We're asking you to come out quietly. You can't shoot it out. We've got this dump surrounded. We've got machine guns and tear gas bombs. Either you step out here or we open fire.'

Johnny turned to Stella, who was pale. He gripped her arm. He said: 'Give me a kiss, baby!'

She tilted her face and kissed him. He said: 'It's been swell knowing you. Don't forget me too soon. Now walk out there an' give yourself up. Don't be afraid. Bats was no account, they won't hang you if you plead self-defence. He was out to attack you: that can be proved by the fact he busted into your room — maybe you'll get a coupla years for manslaughter but no more. Go on, honey . . . '

She said: 'I'm staying with you, Johnny. I won't go — '

'Don't be a nut! You'll be killed . . . '

'I don't want to live if you go. I want to stay with you. I mean that Johnny, I mean it! You can't make me go! Give me a gun!'

He said: 'Go on, get out, fast — '

'No!' She took one of the shot guns from the floor. She came to the windows with him. She said: 'Are there any back windows?'

'No — but be sensible, kid . . . '

'I won't!'

From outside someone called: 'We're coming in, Carter!'

The darkness was shot with flame and lead whizzed towards the flimsy wooden cabin.

They fired themselves, swiveling their guns and distributing their shots. The police were kept at a distance, giving all they had in the way of lead. They could hear bullets whizzing past their heads, but neither Stella nor Johnny flinched.

Johnny, still staring fiercely forward, said: 'Thanks for everything, kid, I got you into this, I guess . . . '

She didn't answer. She wasn't firing any more. He looked round and she was lying on the floor.

In the centre of her forehead was an ugly, blood-smeared hole!

'*Kid!*' He knelt beside her, stared — then he bent and very gently kissed her on the lips.

He got up; he caught a gun in each hand, kicked open the door.

'You hear, coppers? I'm comin' out — firin'!'

He walked out with guns blazing; the fury of hell broke loose and his world dissolved in a cataclysm of orange-hued flashes and bullets . . .

The Guy in the
Wardrobe

Up and down the Bowery there is a citizen who is known to one and all as 'Sloppy Lou.' This Sloppy Lou is such a guy as you would not look at twice if you happened to be a swell Lulu, in fact he is such a character as you would not even look at once!

He is undersized and he has on the side of his nose a wart which is even bigger than the nose itself. His eyes are worked on different strings, and his clothes are always hanging off him as if at any moment he will fall right through them.

In fact, such a spectacle is this guy that twice he has been swept up by local garbage collectors, and has not been sorted out until he has been found squirming on the conveyor belt.

Now it is a fact known to one and all that this character is hit very hard for a tomato by the name of Mitzi Ritzi which performs a strip dance down at Barney's

Bowery Bowl. And mostly guys are very, very sorry for Lou, on account of Mitzi uses him like he was a retriever dog, sending him for this and for that, and taking anything he gives her, but never even so much as giving him a tumble where her heart was concerned. Which is all very sad on account of Lou is quite a nice guy, and very meek, and such a merchant as will never play a lowdown trick on his friends.

He does not see that Mitzi is making a first-class mug of him, in fact he does not see anything when she is around except maybe her figure, which is very cute, and her fancy garters, which she wears for her act, and which have poor Lou well and truly dazzled.

He does not even see that Mitzi has set her trap for a guy called Larry Ayres, who owns the 'Saucy Nineties Club,' at which place Mitzi is very anxious indeed to do her act. But it is very plain to one and all that Lou might as well find him a dame with fallen arches and knock knees, as waste his time chasing Mitzi any longer.

Until one night, when Lou is playing

craps with Chinese Sam and Big Bull, and his lucky streak is in so much that he winds up not only with the respective rolls, but also with their pants and shirts and other personal attire.

Being a nice guy, he gives back the pants so they can get home, and when he comes to count his roll he finds that he has cleaned them out of more than thirty thousand dollars, and he is very pleased about this as it means he will be able to put on a front for Mitzi.

Lou's lucky streak is right in, and he goes on gambling for the next month. When he finally takes a rest he finds he has now got more than eighty thousand bucks to his credit, and is, in fact, a dime millionaire, and then somewhat.

Of course, there are plenty of characters who give Mitzi the tip about this, and Mitzi immediately deserts Larry Ayres and makes seven kinds of play for Lou. Eventually she persuades him to buy out Larry Ayres, and to star her at the 'Saucy Nineties,' and change the name to 'Mitzi's Joint.'

Not long after this it is announced around that Mitzi has very kindly consented to marry Sloppy Lou, and certain characters in these parts walk around with raised eyebrows and puzzled frowns for many days thereafter. And, in fact, until the deed is done, and Lou and Mitzi have settled down in the little apartment over their new club which Lou refers to as 'The Love Nest.'

I see Sloppy Lou in the nightclub one night, and he sits at my table, and before long he becomes very confiding. In fact, he tells me all his troubles, and it now seems he has plenty and then a few.

'Smoky,' he says. 'It is *terrible*, this married life.'

'I would not know about that, Lou,' I tell him. 'How do you mean it's terrible?'

'Smoky,' he moans, 'When I was knee high to a poker table, my old mother says to me like this: 'Lou,' she says, 'When you grow up you must marry and make yourself a comfortable home, and not run wild around and about the town.'

'Also,' continues Lou. 'She gives me to understand that it is very nice to be happily married and that a wife is a very valuable article.

'But,' he goes on. 'This is not the way it is with Mitzi! In fact it is not any way with Mitzi. I am beginning to think,' he adds, wistfully, 'that she marries me for my money.'

'What makes you think anything like that, Lou?' I say.

'You know, Smoky,' he continues, leaning closer, 'I always understood married people share a bedroom . . . but this is not so with Mitzi and me. Ever since the day we are married she insists I have *my own room*, and in fact, do not bother her in *any way whatsoever*. Furthermore, I suspect she puts *sleeping tablets* in my bedtime cup of milk, because I *always* drop off to sleep the very minute I get onto the bed. All this is upsetting me. It seems to me that Mitzi is not being fair with me at all.'

I feel sorry for him, and say: 'Lou, have you, as yet, taken any insurance out on your *life*?'

'Why, no, Smoky. Although Mitzi has once or twice said I should take out a fifty thousand dollar policy.'

'Then don't,' I warn him, 'It is

rumored around the Bowery that the second you take out that policy for Mitzi, Larry Ayres will arrange to have you disposed of some dark night. I am not able to say where I secure this information . . . but it is worth taking note of.'

He looks pained: 'Smoky, Mitzi would not do this to *me*.'

All the same, as he goes away he looks *very* thoughtful.

A week later there is a big scandal up and down the Bowery. It appears that Lou gets tired of being put off by Mitzi, and late one night busts into her room. She is in bed, and Lou goes over and says like this: 'Mitzi, I have come to the end of my rope. Either you are my wife or you aren't. Either you want me or you don't. If not, say so, and I will kill myself here and now.'

Mitzi seems startled at first, then she laughs as he brings out a gun and points it at his head.

'You wouldn't have the nerve, Lou,' she laughs.

'Mitzi,' says Lou. 'I am hearing rumors about town which I do not like in any way whatsoever. They are saying that when I take out the insurance policy on my life that Ayres will have me shot, and then that you and he will marry and live happily on the money I will leave. Is this true? Are you *still seeing* Ayres?'

'Why, Lou,' she says. 'That is most unkind of you to say like that. I have not seen Larry since the wedding.'

'And you do not love him?' insists Lou.

'I love you, Lou, of course.'

'Then,' says Lou. 'I can stay here in future, in this room with you? You will be a good wife to me?'

Mitzi bites her lip, then says, 'Well, no, Lou. I don't love you in *that* way.'

Lou gives a cry, and without another word jerks the gun to his head, pulls the trigger . . . and somehow misses.

But not altogether. For there is a sudden cry from the wardrobe where his bullet has struck, the door opens, and Larry Ayres comes tumbling out, *shot through the heart!*

Lou is dumbfounded, and very upset; and Ayres does not delay, but within two minutes he ups and passes from this world.

Of course there is an inquest, but Lou's story is foolproof. And so shaken is Mitzi that we hear later she has settled down to being a good wife, and doing as she is told.

I am very very happy for Lou, and so are most other guys on the Bowery. In fact, one and all agree that it is a very good job Lou is such a lousy shot.

I do not see Lou again for some months, but one night he comes over to me in Charlie's Bar, and says as under his breath:

'Smoky,' he says, 'I am very grateful for the warning you gave me one night some time ago. So grateful am I that if at any time you need anything, be sure to let me know. It is this way,' he goes on. 'When you tell me about Ayres planning to have me removed, I get very cautious indeed. I wonder what the idea is in Mitzi doping my milk every night, and accordingly I begin to pour it into the coal bin when she is not looking. I find that every night someone comes in, goes up to Mitzi's room, and *stays until morning*. I do not need two guesses to know *who* this someone *is*.

'But I do not want a divorce. I still love Mitzi. I decide that I will give her a final chance . . .

'So when Ayres has gone up one night I go along and knock at her door. I hear her hiss: 'Quick, Larry, it must be that fool! In the wardrobe . . . quick, darling!' I do not wish to embarrass them, so I wait until she says for me to come in. Then I tell her if she does not want me I will shoot myself. She hums and haws and I point the gun at my head and pull the trigger . . . '

'As it turns out, Lou,' I say. 'It was lucky you missed. If you weren't such a lousy shot . . . '

'*Lousy shot?* Smoky, I once won a Silver Cup for shooting at the Small Arms Club. I *never* miss . . . I didn't ever mean to kill myself . . . I fired *past* my right ear into the wardrobe. You see, that was the only way I could make it *look* an accident!'

He smiles and gets up. He says, 'Now I'll have to be getting along. Mitzi is waiting for me . . . '

'Lou,' I says. 'You sure you won't find any more characters in the wardrobe?'

'No,' he tells me, 'I trust Mitzi . . . and anyway, I take care to have the wardrobe removed!'

The Nervous Ghost

The seedy little man approached Clinton Arnold as the latter was about to leave Bishopley Station.

He was a strange contrast to the bluff, red-faced Yorkshire man in the heavy ulster. His long, dark neck hunched miserably on his scrawny shoulders, his nose was raw and running from exposure to the cold. Dewdrops hung from the end of his frosty little moustache.

'I — er — beg your pardon,' he shivered, hugging his coat closer to him. 'But I wonder if — that is — are you, by any chance, going — er — my way?'

Clinton halted and looked at him.

'Which is your way?'

'Er — I'm going along towards — towards Templeton,' said the harassed-looking little man, apologetically. 'But — you see I'm rather nervous of walking alone — ever since that horrible happening at the — the Hall . . . ' He stopped short.

Clinton smiled: 'You can walk with me, certainly.'

'Thank you — that's very kind of you — '

They turned from the station; Sam, the carrier, was loading his wagon with boxes and parcels, the snow falling thickly on to his bent shoulders and the back of his horse.

'Nasty night, Sam.'

'Aye, Mister Arnold. I'm thinkin' I'll have to be moving a sight faster if I'm to get through. Missus wants me 'ome early — there's a party — '

'Hope you enjoy it, and a Merry Christmas, Sam.'

'Same to you sir. Good night.'

Clinton strode on into the teeth of the snowfall, the little man hurrying uneasily by his side.

Clinton smiled — the little man's face was white and nervous, his scrubby moustache twitching furtively, his eyes darting here and there.

'You needn't worry about the ghost, man,' said Clinton, good-humouredly. 'That's an old wives' tale. You don't mean

180

to tell me you actually *believe* there's anything in it?'

The little man shuddered: 'I *do*,' he said fervently. 'I *know* there is. But it isn't altogether the ghost that worries me. It's just the loneliness of the district, that's all. I hate loneliness, don't you?'

'Can't say I ever gave it a thought,' observed Clinton. 'But if you're so nervous why didn't you take a cab — ?'

'I couldn't do that. I *have* to walk — '

Clinton shrugged. 'You can rest easy anyhow. We aren't likely to see any ghosts about — I've walked this way quite a lot and I never saw one yet.'

'But did you ever walk this way at this particular *time*, and on this particular *date*?' breathed the frightened man. 'You know the story, don't you? Gray was a stockbroker in the city, married to a young, pretty woman. One Christmas Eve ten years ago, he thought he'd be detained in town the night, and telephoned his wife to say so. At the last minute he found he could still catch the last train down here — he did. It was a night like this — heavy snow, everything cold and dreary and dark. He came along this very road — reached the Hall where he lived, halfway to Templeton, sneaked in to surprise his wife — *and found her in bed with another man*.

'He lost his senses, I think. Anyway he set on them like a mad man, with an old coal hammer, battered their heads in — then he went upstairs and shot himself. The man lived long enough to tell the tale, the woman was dead when help arrived. James Gray was lying in his room, shot through the left temple. Ever since then they say that each Christmas Eve Gray walks from the station along this lane, and the whole tragedy is reenacted in the empty house.'

Clinton laughed: 'They *always* say that. Forget it. You know what a superstitious bunch these country yokels are. I'm surprised a man like yourself should be taken in by their tales.'

'You don't believe the story?' asked the man.

'I don't. I didn't know James Gray but I hear he was a nervous kind of chap . . . and can you picture a *nervous ghost*?'

'He was nervous,' nodded the little man. 'I knew him well. He was closer to me than anyone — I know that night he just saw red and hardly realized what he was doing. And now — if he's Earthbound and forced to reenact his crime every Christmas Eve — can't you picture his *horror*, his *loathing*? How he must *feel*?'

'I don't think you need worry about that. James Gray left all worries behind when he shot himself. Dead men *don't* come back.'

'That's your opinion. But I can picture only too clearly how he must feel as he hurries along this lane to the derelict Hall — knowing that he has to live that terrible few minutes over again every year for eternity — '

Clinton grew tired of the subject. He pointedly made no further remark. They walked on, and now, through the snow, the black bulk of the empty Hall loomed large. Clinton glanced aside, saw that his companion's face was contorted with terror. He said: 'If it affects you as badly as that let's hurry.'

He bent his head to the snow and pushed forward. He heard the sudden rusty creaking as the Hall gate was opened. He spun about — the little man had left him, had turned into the Hall drive. He was walking rapidly along towards the silent house. Clinton yelled: 'Hey. What . . . '

The little man gained the door, pushed it open on crazy hinges. He vanished into the darkness inside. And suddenly, from the empty house, came shrill, agonized screams of pain. But it was the voice of a *woman*, not a man. Wild curses reached Clinton's ears faintly, more screams — silence. Then — a shot.

Clinton got his legs moving, hurried forward blindly towards the door. He threw it open, went inside. The place was as dark and silent as ever. Empty. He searched puzzledly, from top to bottom.

There was nothing. Not even the little man.

Clinton gave it up. He walked slowly back to the gates. He saw now that only *one* set of footprints marred the whiteness of the snow on the drive. *His own*.

Indecisively he halted outside the gate, looked back. A light came towards him along the lane. Sam's cart jogged to a halt alongside.

'Not 'ome yet, Mister Arnold? Want a lift?'

'I've lost someone,' Clinton explained. 'The little seedy chap who was with me when I left the station. He hasn't passed you, going back, has he?'

Sam scratched his head, looked puzzled. He said: 'Seedy chap? But you was *alone* when you left the station, Mister Arnold. There wasn't no-one with you, that I swear.'

Clinton's fists tightened. He said: 'I — I see. I — possibly I met him *after* I passed you. Yes, that would be it.'

He stole another glance at the dark house behind him, at the one set of footprints in the snow. He said: 'I — eh — I think I'll have that lift, Sam. Gets kind of lonely out here, doesn't it?'

He climbed onto the cart, and it jolted away, leaving the Hall silent, desolate and shunned, behind it . . .

A Sound in the
Doorway

Hilary Marlowe had every reason to be happy and contented with her married life — no reason at all to be dissatisfied. Most women would have surrendered willingly their only pair of nylons to be in her position; tall, fair-haired Harry Marlowe — the eminent sportsman — as a husband; the Marlowe estate, with unlimited grounds, a lake and superb mansion; a staff of maids and footmen to grant her slightest wish; house parties and social events continually taking place.

Yet, somehow, vaguely, Hilary was intensely bored. It was not evident on the surface but it was there, deep inside her — she was bored with the old familiar faces, the parties, the lake, the grounds — even with her husband.

Harry Marlowe had been her first and last affair; she had married when she was only eighteen, and for five years had been perfectly happy with him. Then a small, nagging voice within her had whispered that Harry had cheated her of her fun, her youth. She should have had a dozen boy-friends now, able to pick her ideal man from their ranks, but here she was — married to Harry! Harry, who worshipped her, it was true, but who wasn't exactly her notion of a prince in shining armour.

Everything might have been all right even then, if Harry had had the sense not to bring his old school friend, Tony Blaton, down for a weekend.

Everyone knew Tony Blaton! His name decorated the front of a score of romantic novels — novels which Hilary read with many an inward sigh and tiny pang of regret that her own life had not been fashioned on the lines of one of Tony Blaton's heroines.

She was delighted when Harry turned up one Saturday evening with the celebrated author himself. Tony was not tall; he was of medium height, dark-haired and immaculate. Quite the reverse of Harry, in his rough tweeds; with untidy fair hair ruffled by the wind. Tony's voice was deep and soft; Harry's loud and noisy. Tony's ways were gentle, tender; Harry's very rough. Tony had wistful grey eyes; Harry had jocular blue ones.

Hilary didn't try to deceive herself. She knew, the moment Tony took her hand gently and smiled a greeting, that she was about to fall in a big way. Fall she did — not slowly or gradually, but instantaneously. She was sure that Tony cared for her from little significant remarks he let fall; at least *she* knew they were significant. She threw herself at the young novelist, and waited breathlessly to see whether he would catch!

Her behaviour was obvious to everyone in the house; even the servants realised that she was wrapped up in Tony.

Hilary had no idea she was being so careless until one night, as she was preparing to retire, Harry walked into her bedroom looking rather serious. For a second or two he stood shuffling his large feet uncomfortably. Then —

'Look here, Hilary,' he said self-consciously. 'What's going on between you and Tony?'

'Going on?' said Hilary, continuing to

brush her golden hair. 'How do you mean, dear?'

'Going on!' snapped Harry. 'That's how I mean. Do you fancy I'm blind? Do you think I can't see — that the servants, my guests can't see you're throwing yourself at the man? Good God! You're making an absolute show of yourself — and of me, too!'

Hilary turned in her chair and fixed a frigid eye on her husband.

'Very well!' she stated calmly. 'If you wish to know, I am — er — as you so neatly put it, throwing myself at Tony. Surely there is no need to act like a child, Harry? After all, we aren't silly kids any longer, you know. If I happen to lose my love for you — well, can *you* blame me? All you ever think of is golf, horse-riding, golf again and more golf. Let's be sensible, dear. Tony loves me, and . . . '

'Has Tony told you that?' asked Harry, startled.

'Not in as many words. Yet you must have noticed — since you seem to have been snooping about — that he likes to be near me, takes me for walks in the woods, goes swimming with me in the lake and is always attentive.'

'Ye Gods!' groaned Harry. 'Can't you see that that's merely because he wants to be polite to his best friend's wife?'

'All right, Jealous,' said Hilary with a silvery laugh. 'I expected you to say something like that. Very well, if he doesn't like me, why does he keep coming for weekends?'

'Because he likes me! I've been his friend since we were at college together.'

'Then if you're jealous why not forbid him to come?'

'For the same reason! Do you imagine that I am going to exclude my best friend simply because a little idiot is continually embarrassing him by trying to palm herself off on to him?'

Hilary's eyes were flashing.

'You've said enough, Harry! I shall do as I please — all I want you to do is to give me a divorce when Tony forgets his loyalty to you and asks me to marry him. He will do, I know.'

'You mean that you're going to keep up this silly game? Oh, forget it, Hilary! I was planning a long trip to the South Seas. It would be a second honeymoon for us, dear. Forget what I said — forget Tony, and come along with me.'

'After what you've said tonight I wouldn't go as far as the corner of the street with you, Harry!'

'Don't be silly, Hilary! You know that you don't really love Tony. It's just a silly crush . . . '

'Shut the door after you,' snapped Hilary, with finality.

Harry left the room with a hurt expression in his eyes. The laughter and merriment had gone from them now; only pain remained. He hadn't realised just how big a hold Tony had on his wife. Something had to be done . . . He knew in his heart that Tony would never betray his friendship — or he was almost sure of it!

* * *

Several weekends passed, with Harry still in this unhappy state. Hilary herself, although enjoying her innocent affair with

Tony, was beginning to wish he would not remain so loyal to Harry. She thought that perhaps Harry had been right after all — perhaps Tony would be content to love her secretly, happy in just being near her.

The climax was reached one evening about six weeks after Harry had first spoken to her about it. She had been strolling aimlessly in the garden, when she heard a soft step and turning, saw Tony beside her. His face was grave and serious as he took her arm and his deep, husky voice sent a strange, glowing feeling along her spine.

'Hilary — my dear — I — must talk to you!'

She thrilled with pleasure, for it was the first time he had called her 'dear.'

'Go on, please, Tony. Is it — is it important?'

Tony nodded. Behind his grave expression she could detect the lines of worry and indecision.

'Not here, Hilary. Let's walk as far as the summer house.'

They strolled through the moonlight,

silently, each busy with personal thoughts. Hilary knew the moment was here at last — somehow she felt vaguely disappointed that Tony was, after all, about to betray the trust and esteem in which Harry held him. It was merely a passing thought — it did not recur.

They reached the summer house and entered, quietly.

'Well — Tony dear?' Hilary sounded a little breathless; she was close to him, *very* close. The subtle perfume she used was numbing his senses, she knew. The moonlight was streaming through the glass roof, bathing them in soft enchantment. Then his arms were about her; holding her tightly.

'Oh, what's the good, Hilary? You must know what I wish to tell you — I love you, dear; have done for a long time — and I think you feel the same.'

'I do,' she said simply.

'But — well, there's Harry!'

'He'll give me a divorce, dear; I know he will.'

'It's such a rotten trick . . . You do love me?'

'I could never love any other man,'

she whispered. His lips moved towards hers — for a second she felt a little panicky — then she surrendered. Just one moment more and his lips would be pressed against hers for their first kiss.

That moment never came. There was a sound in the doorway, and they spun round . . .

'Harry!' gasped Hilary. Tony said nothing.

Harry was standing grimly in the doorway. In his hand he held his revolver; the safety catch was off . . .

'Caught you at it, have I?' he asked, unemotionally. There was something strange, deadly about his expression. Hilary shivered.

'I once told you, Hilary, that I'd kill any man who took you from me. Remember? I guess that threat — or boast — call it what you will, holds good.' He looked directly at Tony. 'We've been pals a long time now, Tony. I didn't want to do this — I'm not the type really — but I must! I can't stand the thought of Hilary with anyone else!'

'I know I've been rotten,' said Tony,

desperately. 'But for God's sake, don't shoot, Harry! Hilary means nothing to me. I promise I'll never come near her again! Don't shoot, for Heaven's sake!'

'Sorry,' said Harry shortly. His finger tightened, squeezed . . . The shot echoed through the silent garden, mingling with Hilary's terrified scream. Tony Blaton fell clumsily, a hand pressed to his heart. He gave a convulsive twitch, then lay still.

Harry, holding the smoking gun, crossed over and knelt beside him.

He stood up after a second.

'Through the heart,' he said tonelessly. 'Nice, clean, instantaneous death. It was the least I could do for the poor chap!'

Hilary stood petrified, with open, unblinking eyes. Then suddenly she turned from the still body. Tears streamed from her eyes, coursing down her white face. Harry placed an arm about her and she buried her face against his jacket.

'Oh, Harry!' she sobbed. 'How — how could you? They'll take you — hang you — oh — '

'I know! But that doesn't matter. What

use is life without you, dear? When I saw you no longer wanted me . . . '

'But I do want you! I know now — now you've done this horrible thing. I didn't really want Tony; I know that, too. I want you, Harry . . . '

'Even after — this?'

'Of course! Even after this. I didn't *bargain* for anything like this — if only you had waited — I'd most likely have come to my senses any way. Oh, Harry . . . '

'There may be a chance yet! Quickly, go back to the house and pack a few things. We'll leave on that trip I told you about — the South Seas.'

'But they'll trace you . . . '

'They won't even look for me. I know where I can put — Tony! They'll never find the body. Unless you don't really want to go . . . '

'Oh, I do, I do!'

'Then hurry! I'll be back at the house in a few minutes — by then Tony Blaton will have vanished mysteriously!'

He pushed her towards the door; with one last terrified stare at the dead man she ran along the path . . .

When she had gone, Harry Marlowe lit a cigarette and crossed over to the corpse. 'All right, Tony, old bean,' he grinned. 'You can get up now — must be dashed uncomfortable down there.'

The dead man raised himself on one hand.

'She gone?'

'She has! As you heard, it worked beautifully. She really thought you'd been shot, old man.'

Tony, smiling, raised himself from the floor and carefully dusted his evening dress suit.

'You know, Harry, all the time I was waiting for you to pull that trigger I was as windy as the Devil. Thought you might have been mixed up and put real bullets in it instead of blanks.'

Harry answered with a smile: 'No fear! I'm blessed if I'd ever have the nerve to kill anyone!'

'Surely you aren't going on letting her think you're a murderer?'

'Hardly! I'll let her worry for a few days. Then I'll tell her. She will have learned a valuable lesson by then, I hope.'

'She'll be furious!'

'No. I don't think so. She'll be too relieved to know that I'm not a murderer, after all. You see it was the only way to bring her to her senses. If I'd said she hadn't to see you again, she'd have been worse than ever. At the same time I knew you really didn't want her — that's why I asked you to do this — because if *you* didn't, I still did.'

They strolled along the path towards the house.

'You'd better hang on here till we've started, Tony. It wouldn't do to let her spot you at present.' The two men clasped hands.

'There's just one thing,' said Tony. 'Suppose she *had* preferred me after all? What would you have done then? She'd have hated you!'

'In that case,' said Harry, thoughtfully, 'I should have reloaded the gun with real ammunition, then . . . '

'You mean you really would have shot . . . '

'Myself!' answered Harry, quietly. 'So long, Tony!'

His tall figure vanished into the house, where an anxious Hilary awaited him.

Gavoti Was Yellow

'Attention, ladies and gents! This is your old news maestro on the air again, bringing you the latest and best in comments on the news of the day.'

The sharp, whip-like voice of Denny Davis, ace newscaster on the *Krinkly Kornflakes Hour* which was broadcast over the LXB network every Friday night, came snapping through the countless loudspeakers in millions of American homes.

People of all classes ceased what they were doing to listen, for Denny Davis was always sure to have some new slant on the current news of the day. In three short years he had become almost a national institution!

'Flash! What famous actress, now featured in a Broadway play, is getting around with what prominent playboy who has already divorced his five previous wives . . .?'

Many of the listeners grinned. The inference was obvious to them.

' . . . Special Flash! Today the murderer of Luke Shore, prominent Wall Street business magnate, was apprehended, and after Chief of Police Nichols had used a little gentle persuasion, confessed to the killing! This means that Alex Gavoti, the well-known racketeer who was accused of the killing, will be free to leave the lodgings Uncle Sam has been providing for him, without a stain on his murky character. You folks will remember that I told you *two months ago*, when Gavoti was roped in, that I didn't think he was guilty.

'Why? Because I happen to know his record! Gavoti never kills himself! He employs one of his mob to do the rubbing-out jobs for him. He's much too yellow, folks, to try murder! In fact, I put it on record here and now that Gavoti is about the biggest coward among present-day mobsters. The mere sight of a gun frightens the wits out of him — and if it happens to be in the hands of an enemy, I hear tell he just — swoons! His record speaks for itself! A record of dirty, gutless crimes which, although arranged by him, left him sitting high and dry while his pals took the raps . . . So if he's listening to this he'll know there's one American citizen who is *not* afraid of him and his thugs . . . You hear that, Yellow-Belly Gavoti?'

Davis's listeners gave murmurs of excitement. For the radio columnist had just openly insulted one of gangdom's biggest and most terrifying figures.

' . . . That's all for this evening, folks, but I'll be on the air again next Friday with a fresh basinful of what makes the world go round — until then, this is your own snoopy Denny Davis saying so long . . .'

In the studio, the red light winked and the technicians removed the recording from the turntable.

'Gosh,' exclaimed one as he carefully packed the recorded disc away. 'He sure gave Gavoti hell, huh?'

His companion nodded. 'Yeah! But he wants to watch out for himself! These big noises gotta way of eliminating fresh guys like him.'

'Say,' inquired the other, who was new at the studio. 'Why doesn't he come down here an' speak personally, instead of sending down a dictaphone recording?'

'He gets 'mike fright' bad. The poor guy don't like the idea of gettin' all tongue-tied in the middle of his broadcast, and if he speaks in person he always does. He owns a little dump down on Long Island an' mostly he stays there all the time. His stooges, who circulate over the States, collect all his news for him — he just records it, packs it along and we re-record it an' put it on the air.'

'What a racket,' breathed the new hand. 'What a racket!'

* * *

'O.K., boys,' grunted Alex Gavoti as the dark, bullet-proof car turned into a quiet stretch of road in a lonely district of Long Island. 'This is it!'

His companions, Lippy Small and Eduardo Calloni, two of his mob, nodded. Calloni stopped the car; Small brought out a forty-five, flipped the chamber to see if it were loaded and ready for action, then handed it to Gavoti.

'You sure it's safe, boss?' said Calloni, apprehensively.

'Safe?' Gavoti sneered. 'I thought Davis said I was the one who was yellow? Seems he was wrong — anyway he'll find out.' He grinned, gripped the forty-five tightly and thumbed back the safety catch. 'Sure it's safe,' he added. 'It's three months since Davis made that crack about me in his programme — he's most likely forgotten about it himself by now — an' if he hasn't, the cops have.

'Anyway, they won't be able to make a charge if we work it right an' take care there's no leads for 'em — they never managed to make a rap stick to me yet!' he boasted.

The three slid out of the car and glanced up and down the dark, deserted street.

The house in front of them, entirely surrounded by trees, was only a small affair. They had discovered that Denny Davis lived there entirely alone, without even a servant. The cook and housekeeper came early each day and left at seven, so that it left a clear field for the killing of Denny Davis.

'Stay in the car, Lippy,' said the

racketeer. 'Keep the engine runnin', and keep a look out for cops!'

Lippy nodded and climbed back behind the wheel. The other two pushed open the gate, commenced to creep up the shadowy drive.

To their right they could see a lighted window. Within this room, seated at a desk with his back towards them, was their proposed victim. He was resting with his elbows on the desk, his head in his hands.

Calloni picked up a stone, flung it through the wide French windows. As the crash of broken glass shattered the stillness, Davis turned round, directing from his keen grey eyes an annoyed glance at the window.

'What the hell . . . ?' the gangsters heard him mutter. He stood up, came curiously towards the window, opened it and peered out . . .

Gavoti stepped from behind a tree, gun held menacingly in his right hand.

'Get inside,' he snarled. Calloni joined him.

Denny Davis didn't argue. He had a

feeling that this was going to be one scoop some other newscaster would break to the listening world. He backed into his study, hands held high. Gavoti and Calloni followed him in.

They stood just inside the windows; Gavoti's features twisted in a sneer.

'Now how about it, Mister?' he demanded. 'In case you wonder what it's all about, my name's Gavoti — this here's Ed. Calloni, one of my boys, an' Lippy Small's waitin' outside in the getaway car. So you see, Mister Snoopy Davis, you handed yourself quite a nice little parcel of trouble when you told the world I was too yellow to kill any guy — '

'So you're going to prove to me that you're not, eh?' Denny was quite calm, betrayed no panic. He knew better than to imagine that any plea he might make would have any effect on the brutal-faced man confronting him.

'We are — at least, I am! Ordinarily I'd leave the job to Calloni here — he's my strong-arm. But you call for a little special an' personal attention, Mister . . . Here it is!'

His face did not change as he pulled his index finger back on the trigger . . . three times . . .

Davis didn't yell, didn't make a sound. His knees buckled as the hot lead smacked home in his stomach; he did a Brodie on to the carpet . . .

'Okay,' grated Gavoti. 'That's it!'

'Hold it, boss,' Calloni told him. 'You ain't intendin' to leave this guy here like this, are yuh?'

'Sure, why not? He took it in the stomach — he'll croak within half an hour an' it won't be too pleasant a death . . . '

'Yeah,' agreed Calloni. 'And inside that half hour he might make the 'phone, call the cops, and tell them who done it!'

Gavoti realised his stooge was right. Once more his gun came up and put an end to Davis' squirming and faint moaning.

Then the two killers returned down the pathway, wiped away any fingerprints which might have been on the gate, and crammed into the car . . .

'Fire away, Lippy,' grunted Gavoti. 'We're all clear an' the cops'll never pin this on us in a hundred years . . . '

' . . . so don't forget, ladies and gentlemen,' said the announcer, 'that Krispy Kornflakes are the finest that money can buy . . . And now — as you all know, Denny Davis, who has given you all the latest on the latest in this weekly hour, for three years now, was brutally killed two days ago at his Long Island home.

'What you were unaware of, however, was that Denny recorded all his talks and that we down here rerecorded them and broadcast them to you folks, his fans. Well, you probably thought you'd heard Denny Davis on the air for the last time. But while going through his effects, after the police investigation, his brother found his last talk to you people. It was a dictaphone recording, still in place on the machine and, on trying it, Harry Davis found that the opening remarks were addressed to you folks.

'So he rushed it down to us, feeling that it would be a fitting tribute to pay to a great radio personality if we played it for the last time . . . We haven't had time to re-record it for you — so here it is on the original roll . . . '

'Attention, ladies and gents!' came the sharp tones of the deceased newscaster. 'This is your old news maestro bringing you the latest on the latest . . . Two days ago a certain big-time oil well owner divorced his wife! Grounds were given as incompatibility, but between you and me and the microphone, I have learned that . . . ' There was a sudden shattering sound of breaking glass and the voice stopped.

The recording ran on.

'What the hell . . . ?' muttered Denny's voice. The eager listeners heard him rise from his desk, heard his steps crossing the room. Then another voice suddenly snapped into the record.

'Get inside!' it snarled.

Silence for a minute, then: 'Now how about it, Mister? In case, you wonder what it's all about, my name's Gavoti . . . this here's Ed. Calloni, one of my boys, an' Lippy Small's waitin' outside in the get-away car . . . '

Thunderstruck, the studio staff and thousands of listeners breathlessly waited, ears glued to their receivers. They heard the full conversation — they heard three shots, then Denny's faint moans . . . Calloni's suggestion that Davis might 'phone, and the three final shots which finished Denny Davis off . . .

★ ★ ★

Gavoti was the first to admit that it had been very unfortunate that Denny had been recording his broadcast the evening they had called on him.

But for that . . .

As it was, of course, Gavoti paid the supreme penalty together with his side-kicks . . . and in the end it was proved that Denny Davis was right when he said Gavoti was a yellow rat . . . for that worthy had to be carried forcibly to the chair, kicking and screaming . . .

THE END